A SOLITARY SMILE

A Novel *on Einstein*

BEELINE PRESS
NAPLES, FLORIDA
2019

A Solitary Smile

ISBN 978-1-64540-030-1

A SOLITARY SMILE

A Novel *on Einstein*

David R. Topper

For
Martin J. Klein
1924 – 2009

"Here I sit, in order to write ... something like my own obituary."

—From the first line of Albert Einstein's autobiographical essay, drafted in 1946.

Table of Contents

1. **Late-morning**.. 1

2. **Mid-afternoon** 46

3. **Late-afternoon**.. 105

4. **Evening**.. 145

5. **Late-night**... 171

Afterword... 191

Acknowledgments 195

1. Late-morning

"Falling in love is not at all the most stupid thing that people do – but gravitation cannot be held responsible for it." —Einstein, 1933

*Oy shit, not again – gotta run, fast, faster. My dim-witted classmates, chasing me, catching up. Ah, our stupid teacher, bringing a large nail to school and bellowing about Jesus on the Cross – proclaiming that **this** was the nail used by the Jews to crucify The Lord. Ah, crap. These brainless lads believe this rubbish, and so here is the one small Jew in the class running home from school, again. Will they catch me this time?*

Oy, not again – that dream. Not that dreadful memory. Must have dozed off. Still a trauma. Okay, wake up. Forget it.

But I can't. Any disturbing dream lingers in my mind, even after I am awake. The image stays, many minutes – so that, if I close my eyes again, I return directly to the dream. Thus, closing my eyes, I am back to my childhood, running home from school. Ah.

I always hated the approach of Easter, every year. When was that? How many years? Humm, I like doing math in my head: let's see, I was about ten years old, so that means it happened about sixty-six years ago. Long ago, but still traumatized.

Ah, what woke me up? What was that noise? Something woke me from that dream? Why was I dozing off, again? Can't seem to stay awake to write this letter. I guess my comfy study chair is just *too* comfy. What *was* that noise? Humm, what is all the fuss, coming from downstairs? In the kitchen? Women laughing, who is that giggling? Ah, Miss Dukas. What were they doing in the kitchen this morning when I came up here to work? Oh, yes, Margot was making a beef stew in that new quick cooking device she bought on sale. Uh, a pressure cooker. How did they ever patent such a thing?

—Dukas, Dukas, what is all that racket about? Huh? Dukas, where are you? Are you not in the kitchen?

Ow, another sharp pain in my gut. Ah, the aneurysm. I'm afraid this swollen aorta behind my stomach is going to kill me one of these days. Ha, I guess I have my own an internal pressure cooker – yet with much pain, and often even vomiting. Last fall it had me bedridden for weeks, but by the new year I was back to work on my unified field theory, plus working on my intermittent critiquing of politics and society, especially here in America.

—Professor, sorry for the din. We had an accident in the kitchen, just as I predicted. I told Margot not to buy that *Presto* gadget that is all the rage. The contraption scares me to death. With that little jiggling thing on the top, always letting off steam. It is like a hissing and spitting wild animal. Well, it blew, and now there is beef stew on the ceiling. The gardener heard the blast and he is on a ladder helping us to clean up the mess.

—That jiggling thing is a pressure release value, apparently poorly designed. Remember, I worked at a patent office for several years in Bern. I am not a just physicist with his mind always in the clouds, which I know is my stereotype. Uh, of course, sometimes I *do* behave that way. You know, that reminds me: one day, I was walking home with a colleague from the Institute, and he told me some profound idea that had *never* occurred to me – well, I was so awestruck by the idea that I stopped completely in my tracks, and just stared off into space pondering the thought. However, the problem was, at that very time we were crossing a busy street. And so: there we were, the two of us in the middle of the street, with cars weaving around and horns honking – none of which I heard, since my mind was, eh, in the clouds. Eventually my friend was able to steer me to the curb, alive – as you can see. So, yes, I suppose I do come by the stereotype honestly. Nonetheless, I am not always that way. Indeed, I grew up in my father's electrical shop with motors and dynamos and all kinds of interesting gadgets. He wanted me to be an engineer. Indeed, I hold a number of patents for things I designed.

—Yes, professor, I know all that. Maybe therefore you should look at the jiggling thing. Redesign it? Eh?

—More likely, the jiggling thing was used improperly by my step-daughter. And so, presto, it went kaboom – ah, *Presto*, indeed.

—I am afraid it is rather dangerous. I feel rather silly for laughing so much. But, in fact, it was all very funny, that's why I was laughing so hard. I'll probably dream tonight of beef on the ceiling. Yet, still, some-one could get hurt.

—Well, yes, maybe you are right. But then, ow, my gut again.

—Professor, I am worried. We should do something. Maybe you should not eat the beef tonight.

—Don't worry. I am getting used to this. Yes, this aneurysm will kill me, someday. But I am no vegetarian. I know that since my health problems after the First War, I was on a strict diet, often lacking in meats. And Elsa diligently looked over me with her special cooking. But I still enjoy many a meaty meal, and I am not going to skip the stew after this hullabaloo with the pressure cooker. Well, the pressure cooker in my gut will eventually kill me. So, what? I've already lived over twice as long as Mozart.

—Professor, you have become so morbid lately.

—Speaking of morbid, mortuary, death. There is this condolence let-ter that I am trying to write, when kaboom.

—I will leave you alone to write that letter to the Besso family, while I go downstairs and help clean up.

—Okay, you are probably needed in the kitchen.

Sigh.

Trying to write this condolence letter triggers memoires of the past.

Oh, Albert, where would you be without Dukas, Miss Helen Dukas, your secretary since 1928, now your housekeeper too? She has devoted her entire life to you and your family, ever since you hired her. She, along with your step-daughter, Margot, are your daily companions.

Ah, yes, Besso, you are so right. I would be lost without them, especially Dukas. After I became a celebrity in the 1920s I was flooded with mail. I could not keep up, I needed a secretary. I went through several, until Miss Dukas came along. It was a Friday the 13th, her lucky day. She then moved with us to Princeton, in 1933; and when Elsa died, she took over the household chores. She will surely outlive me, and keep up with organizing my archives, estate, and the house – long after I am gone.

Sigh.

So, back to the letter. My old friend, my best friend, Besso, he also lived over twice as long as Mozart.

Ah, Mozart – classic, ideal music: pure, graceful, elegant, ordered, simple, balanced, harmonious music. Unlike Beethoven, who *created* music, Mozart, as it were, *found* music – almost as if it were at the heart of the universe, waiting to be revealed. Yes, I see his music as a reflection of the inner beauty of the universe, like my search for the inner harmony of the physical universe. In fact, as I get older, I feel I am experiencing such beauty and truth in their purest forms.

Sigh.

But my life is depressing too. I no longer can play my violin. Although I still doodle on the piano almost daily. It puts me in touch with the harmony of the universe – or, at least, I still try to get in touch.

Um, that reminds me: the other day, one of the notes on a page of music I was playing began moving. What? Ah, it was a small black bug walking among the notes, writing a different melody. Improving Mozart! What's to improve? Perfection: like the universe itself.

Ah, and Spinoza! What was it I always quote about him – that solitary Jewish philosopher from Holland? Ah, yes: that God is revealed in the order and harmony of all that exists in the universe. Yes, Spinoza told the truth, and his religious community excommunicated him for it.

Spinoza, Mozart, 17th & 18th centuries: order, harmony. Did I ever think of them paired like this before? I must have, sometime. Maybe not. Humm. Perhaps my old noggin is not so rusty after all? Miss Dukas says that I am as sharp as ever, but – I know, I know – she says what she thinks I want to hear. She really patronizes me, ah, but then she reprimands me too, occasionally. Rather like a surrogate wife, I guess.

Humm, Dukas: such a matronly persona. Pleasant face, dark hair parted to the side – not too long, but not short either, covering the ears. No aura of sensuality. Wears simple loose blouses with long skirts, or (most of the time around the house) long and dumpy housecoats. I suspect she was a virgin when we hired her, and still one today, maybe? Ah, but where would I be without her?

Sigh.

I relax in my comfy striped chair, with a blanket over my legs and lap, and look out through the large window in my study. Being on the second floor in the back of the house, I get a marvelous view on the garden – and the weather. Um, I love this bright and roomy study, with its simple, functional décor, and wall-to-wall carpeting. The large table in the center was salvaged from Berlin; otherwise a Nazi would have pilfered it. Elsa and I were delighted to get it back. Yes, she made a wonderful choice in picking this house, after we moved from Hitler's Germany to America. It was, I believe, August 1935 that we moved into this modest house at 112 Mercer Street. A two-story white-painted house, with a veranda and green shutters, about a century old on a tree-lined street. Elsa somehow was able to get some of her furniture out of Berlin and transported here through Nazi checkpoints; and so, she furnished this home in her heavy bourgeois style, except for my study. Um, I refused to let the heavy antique furniture in here. Ug, too Victorian. Except for the table.

What I *did* like were the changes she made to this room that is now my study and office. She opened the back wall with the huge window, giving me this grand view of the garden. Ah, praise this large window: Elsa called it a bay window. Today my splendid view of the garden shows the early spring flora unhurriedly greening after the longish winter. I sit looking, not into, but as if *within* the garden surrounded with trees: elms, maples, weeping willows, a grape arbor. The other walls of the room are filled with the floor-to-ceiling bookshelves she had built for me to clutter up: so many books, journals, manuscripts, and mail – seemingly endless mail. Chico feels sorry for me, and he takes it out on the mailman – barking nastily at him when he can.

Ah, I love this room. I see almost all visitors here, only using the living room for special occasions.

Sigh.

It's foggy and drizzling. Unpleasant day, very unpleasant, and so I stayed home from the Institute today. Plus, I need to write that condolence letter. Rain began last night. Winds up to 14 miles per hour; expected to be gustier today. It is 40-degrees this morning, 36-degrees last night when I went to bed. I was always keen about numbers – as long as I can remember. I think I mean that in two ways, humm. I keep track of these things from my radio dial tuned to the weather station. For my seventieth birthday Oppenheimer and the Institute gave me a high-fidelity phonograph machine; and, as well, they gave me an FM radio and had an antenna installed on my roof, so I can listen to symphony concerts from New York. He does not know that I use the radio to keep track of the weather too.

Oh, yes, Oppenheimer, J. Robert Oppenheimer, Director of the Institute for Advanced Study in Princeton, New Jersey. Your boss. Famous for wearing that ragged Stetson western hat, and carrying a pipe, like you – I refer to the pipe, like you, not the hat. You still see him, even though you are retired from the Institute. Yes?

Well, Michele, I still smoke my pipe, even though Elsa struggled tirelessly to get me to quit. And, yes, I still go regularly to the Institute, although officially I am retired. Humm, Oppenheimer, a thin and lanky body, a dominant presence in a room, so much so that he appears to be a lot taller than he is, whereas he is not much taller than me. And I am rather short. Oh yes, that hat, it is part of his persona. His nickname is Oppie, what a silly name. I am embarrassed saying it. So, besides calling him Oppenheimer, I started calling him J. Robert; then J. Rob; and now just J.R. Oppenheimer, both mysterious and tragic. Ah, I think he is pissed off at me for donating all my papers and things to the Hebrew University in Jerusalem, and not to the Institute. The University will get

7

everything sometime after I die. Well, actually, when Dukas dies too. Humm, death, again.

Sigh.

Death thoughts, as I compose a letter of condolence. Sitting in my study, peering out my back window, and thinking of, ah, something about those elms, maples, and weeping willows – inviting deep contemplation, or just any sort of daydreaming. The large thermometer, mounted on the window frame, easily viewed, so I can read off the temperature. Numbers, numbers, again. One of the stereotypes of scientists like me, obsessed with the quantitative. In this case, it is true, well, uh, sort of.

Frankly, I am usually only interested in numbers if they are attached to physical things – temperature, speed, volume, weight, and the like. Not numbers the way mathematicians think of them: in their pristine, remote, abstract state. I think it was Bertrand Russell who said that a major insight in his life took place in his childhood when he realized that three balls, three pounds, and three ideas had something in common – the number three. He instantly realized that numbers exist independently of everything in existence, and even out of existence. Of course, I too appreciate this abstract nature of mathematics, but in a different way. Anyway, it is *all* there in my general theory of relativity.

So, I like numbers that are yoked to the world. Real stuff: to be seen, felt, measured, quantified, that sort of thing. An abstraction, yes, but linked to the universe, the physical universe. Um, real stuff. It began when I was young. It is the way engineers think of numbers. My father wanted me to be an engineer, but I become a physicist – yet, I appreciate the engineering viewpoint. I never fully lost it.

Humm, reminds me of Russell and math again. I recall him telling me that he once worked on an important mathematical problem in his head while he was having sex with a woman. I think it was the wife of a colleague, but I'm not sure how that is relevant to anything, and even why this just came into my mind. Except, that it *is* about the power of abstract thinking and a disconnection with the material world. I mean, how much more material can you get than the act of sexual intercourse? Humm, I forgot to ask him if it helped him solve the problem.

Besso, my best friend, you knew me. We talked about sex as well as physics. Yes, we scientist/engineer types have such desires. I am seen today as a sort of secular saint, with a halo of white hair. But if they – what here in America are called the average Joes – only knew how much sex played a role in my life, would they be surprised. Yes, even Einstein: my mind was not always in the clouds. What else do these Joes *not* know about me? What did you think, Michele? Humm.

So, thinking of a math problem while having sex. No, I don't believe I ever did what Russell said he did! No, numbers and the world were always yoked for me. Humm, yoked, tied, bondage, a good word. *Of Human Bondage*, did I read that book? Somerset Maugham; he took the phrase from Spinoza. His original title was from Isaiah, "Give unto them beauty for ashes." But *Beauty for Ashes* was already the title of a published book. So, Maugham went to Spinoza's *Ethics,* Part IV: *Of Human Bondage, or the Strength of the Emotions.* How do I know these things? A lifetime of reading and thinking, no doubt – and corresponding with smart people. Ah, so many letters over the years. So, so many. Um, it is going to drive the historians who are putting together my archives crazy.

The late-morning fog is lifting. The drizzle continues, the dampness seeps into my house. A chill: I should have put on socks today. I rarely do. The act of dressing oneself is simpler without socks. Like shaving

9

with the same soap that you wash your face with, all it once. Or, like one theory of space for both electricity and gravity – yes, my unified field theory. Still working on this. Ah, a blanket covers my lap and legs – comfort, um, my baggy pants, conducive for writing a letter of condolence.

My good friend Michele Angelo Besso, dead. He was a bit shorter than me. Handsome, like me, as a youth. He had thick dark very curly hair, with a full curly beard. As he aged, it all turned white, also like me. Um, he would be eighty-two in a few months. I am now only seventy-six, well "only" is a relative term. With how I feel, I will never catch up with Besso's eighty-one years. Humm, relative, indeed. Besso helped me with my relativity theory. I need to write a condolence letter to his son, Viro, and his sister, Bice.

Sigh.

How to begin? Start with numbers – a date. Today, Monday, March 21, 1955. Um, March 21, Bach's birthday. J. S. Bach, the father. His many sons were musicians, but the father was the best. Baroque music, just before Mozart. His father was a musician, but here the *son* was the better musician. My son, Hans Albert, an engineer, not as famous as me, well who could be? Poor lad, stuck with the Einstein name. In reality, yoked with it. Ah, yoked again. The bondage of the Einstein name. But Hans Albert is a better husband and father than I was – much better, ah, much, much better. OK, enough. Well, um, posterity should know that I was no model father, or husband. Poor Hans Albert, my father would have been happy with a grandson as an engineer, but he was dead by then. Ah, well.

I very much was *not* a good father to my children. Why not? Today photographers are tripping over themselves trying to get pictures of me surrounded by cute kids. A sweet little girl sitting on Einstein's lap is a prize shot. Also, children from all over the world send me letters and missives, and I even answer some of them. I seem to have more affection for other people's children than my own. Humm, another one of those Einstein contradictions, I suppose.

Sigh.

So, back to the letter of condolence. March 21, ah, the spring equinox: equal daytime and nighttime. The first day of spring, and people think the weather should quickly change because it is spring. But the equinox has nothing – absolutely nothing – to do with the weather, which differs all over the world. The spring equinox is about astronomy. When the sun's annual motion through the ecliptic crosses the celestial equator. That's why the daytime equals nighttime. Actually, this is where the word "spring" comes from, since the sun springs up across the sky's equator – and, incidentally, in the "fall" it falls below the sky's equator. The two terms have nothing to do with flowers springing up from the ground or leaves falling from the trees down here on earth. Yes, it is contrary to the conventional earthly explanation of spring and fall. So, it is actually about celestial events, up there in the sky, in the heavens. Ah, the realm of order and perfection as acknowledged by Spinoza, and shown by me in my general theory of relativity to have a mathematical regularity.

I learned basic astronomy at the Zurich Polytechnic where I first met Michele. When? Around 1897. We called the school the Poly. Besso just died on March 15th. Um, the day after my birthday. Ha, my birthday, last week: reporters hounded me, and so I put myself under house arrest. I am tired of answering stupid questions, the same stupid questions. "No, I have not yet found the secret to the universe – but when I do, you will be the first to know!" However, I enjoyed the visit of Oppenheimer, who brought some phonograph records for this birthday lad. Yes, J.R. is trying to move my tastes in music beyond Mozart, and into the 19th century.

Besso: his birthday is coming up in May, on the 25th. He was born in 1873 in Zurich but grew up in Italy. More numbers. When we met, he had already graduated from the Poly and was a mechanical engineer. He certainly was someone who also liked numbers in things. Like me, Jewish, and easy going, but too easy going, and lacking in ambition – I was the opposite, very different personalities, but we got along swimmingly. Ah, I called him a *schlemiel*, that Yiddish expression for someone who usually screws things up. Later we worked together at the Patent office in Bern. I got him the job, I believe; well, I recommended him. It was a nice "thank you" for his help with my relativity theory, yes?

Oh, Michele, you just beat me to the grave. I guess I immortalized you when I thanked you for your help with what became my special theory of relativity – in that long paper of 1905 about motion, space, and time. I can't believe I did not name anyone else in the paper. No famous physicist, past or present. Just, "my friend and colleague, M. Besso" to whom "I am indebted for many a valuable suggestion." What suggestions? I cannot remember. Something about the concept of time, the relativity of time, I suspect. We talked about trying to explain the theory to a general audience.

Oh, the drizzle has stopped. The gardener Miss Dukas hired is pruning branches that died over the winter. It is spring, despite the cool dampness and drizzle. Ah, yes, soon the warmer springtime sun will bring forth new life, reminding me that something eternal lies beyond reach of the hand of fate and of all human delusions. Just as my scientific work puts me in touch with the realm of infinity and beyond. Well, for now, the gardener is pruning out dead branches. Um, pruning, dead branches. Death.

Death, Besso. Oh, yes, Michele, and the condolence letter I am writing to your family. Who's left? Your wife died before you. When? Near the end of the last war. 1944? She was a Winteler.

I lived with the Winteler family in the year spent studying in the canton school in Aarau. I was preparing myself to qualify for entrance to the Poly, which was one of the best schools in Europe at the time. I had flunked the written entrance exams. Wait: I only flunked the non-science and non-math parts. And, anyway, I was much too young, only sixteen, whereas most students took the test at eighteen. So, why was I taking it at such an early age?

Well, I must be honest with myself here. I had dropped out of German high school. Yes, I was a high-school dropout. Ah, but I had an excuse: I was depressed. Very much so, I was indeed depressed. My father's electrical business went bust and the family was forced to move from Munich, where we lived since I was an infant, to an uncle living in Italy near Milan. They took Maja, my sister, with them – but not me. I was supposed to stay and finish school. Well, I did finish the math curriculum, and even got a letter from my math teacher that I had completed everything. How utterly scrupulous of me – if, I may say so.

Lucky me: the Swiss Poly didn't require a completed high school degree – and, as I recall, that letter from the math teacher was a factor in my taking the Poly entrance exams. I did so well on the math and science parts that the school director told my father that I should spend a year doing make-up work at Aarau before applying again.

Um, what was it that I wrote a few years ago when reminiscing on that *interregnum* year at the canton school? "It made an unforgettable impression on me, thanks to its liberal spirit and the simple earnestness of the teachers who based themselves on no external authority." This school at Aarau was a perfect place for someone of my persuasion, particularly because of my aversion to authority, of all kinds. That year at Aarau was probably the first time I ever liked school. Yes, it surely was.

And, ah, the Winteler family. What a progressive and congenial family of Protestant Christians. Jost, the father, a splendid teacher at the school. Pauline, the mother; I quickly called them Papa and Mommy. And the daughters: Marie and Anna and, humm, cannot remember the third one's name. Of course, Pauline was also my mother's name, so I had two mommy Paulines.

Oh yes, Marie, my first love. She really fell for me. I kissed her on the neck, up and down – slowly, v-e-r-y slowly, and she fell apart. Collapsed in my arms, as I licked her ear lobe. I believe it was her first erotic kiss from a boy. Yes, she really fell for me. And I for her. What did I call her? Ah, "My naughty little angel." Well, geez, I was just a teenager.

Michele, do you remember her? She was your wife's sister? Humm, it is extraordinary what I think of when I talk to myself – um, to *you* – in this way. Plus: I am able to retroactively reprimand myself. Yes, how interesting this daydreaming is. Sort of like talking to a muse. Or thinking about thinking. A switch in the brain – perhaps like changing the font in a written text?

We played duets together: Marie on the piano and me on the violin. Just as I did with my mother too. For Marie and I, music gave us much pleasure. She thought it would lead to marriage, for Marie was smitten more than I. Much more. Too much more. She still believed that we would be married long after I, uh – what word should I use? Oh, as they say here in America – I guess I "dumped" her. Humm.

Sad Marie. After I left Aarau for Zurich, I realized I had hurt her badly and wrote a letter to her mother – a "Dear Mommy" letter, honestly – explaining what happened. Ah, I don't think I did a very good job in justifying my actions. I was pretty pathetic. Yes, I was. I tried to explain to her mother that I did not realize that Marie was much more sensitive than I, especially when I was sending her my dirty laundry to clean, while I was already involved with a new girlfriend at the Swiss Poly. I blamed my lack of insight into these human matters on the strenuous work I was doing in physics, as (I said) I was probing into God's nature. In retrospect, I was, in fact, doing just that – as I now realize after having become famous. But still, it was a lame excuse at the time – after all, I was just a student.

Sigh.

Poor Marie. I'm sure she got over me, in time. Yet, I wonder what happened to her?

Poor Marie
          Marie
                    Marie
                              Marie

—What? Marie, is that you?
—Albert, my sweet Albert, it's been so long.
—Where have you been? What happened to you? Have you had a happy life?

15

—Well, Albert, I married and had two sons, but later divorced. I was not happy. The war was dreadful and I wanted to immigrate to America.

—But you were in Switzerland and you were not Jewish.

—It was still awful, and I wrote you asking for money. I heard that you were helping refugees and I thought you might get me and my lads out of Europe.

—It is true. Miss Dukas and I ran a little refugee office out of the home. We were helped by our friend Otto Nathan. I called my cluttered desk my "lawyer's desk." And the three of us did save lives, many I suspect. But you? I do not recall hearing from you.

—I wrote two, maybe more, letters. No reply.

—Miss Dukas, my secretary, always opened my mail and often discarded things she thought were useless or would make me upset. I did, and still do, get much mail from charlatans and cranks. But I always reprimanded her for censoring my personal mail. If I had only known.

—No matter. Too late now. I spend occasional visits in sanatoriums. I am not well, mentally, emotional problems and such, you know. I never recovered from the murder of my mother, I believe.

—Where are you, now?

—Albert, can you not see? I am here, for you. Now. Even though I was the prettiest of the three Winteler girls – everyone said so – you dumped me because I would not give you the physical pleasures you desired, and you went instead to that Serbian girl. The most I would do was to give out the pleasure of our making music together. But it is not too late to make up for what happened. Here, see, this is what you wanted me to show you, oh, so many years ago – and this. Here I am sweet Albert, come, come, come – ah, touch me, here.

—Why you naughty little, oh ...

—Dukas! Where are you? Miss Dukas, come. What is that banging noise? It just woke me up?

—Sorry Professor, it is the gardener in the basement making something. After helping to clean up the kitchen, he went into the basement, since the rain started again. Say, you had a curious little smile on your face as you were sleeping. I was wondering, oh, you dropped your pad of paper when you dozed off. Good thing you held onto your fountain pen. We would have had a mess to clean up again. Remember?

—Tell me. Did I get a letter from a Marie Winteler in the early 1940s asking for help?

—What makes you ask? Were you dreaming about our refugee work?

—No, um, oh, yes, yes, the refugee work. *Oy, she is so intrusive*.

—Why on earth would you be dreaming about that! And why would that make you smile?

—I always scolded you for censoring my mail. Dukas, are you now going to censor my dreams too? *Ah, infinitely intrusive*.

—I was trying to protect you.

—Was there something from a Marie Winteler?

—Perhaps, there was so much pleading.

—What, pray tell, are you going to do after I die? You will have little control over this, since all my papers and everything about my work – all of it, is donated to the Hebrew University in Jerusalem. It's in my will.

—I will do as you have directed, professor. Not to worry. Now, I have today's mail to sort. It just arrived, since I hear Chico barking his special mailman bark.

—Go, but just open it. No censoring, hear?

Michele, where was I before that dream? Dreams, daydreams, dreams within daydreams, humm. Where was I?

Oh, yes, Marie. Marie: I wonder if she is still alive? Her sister, Anna, married my best friend, Besso.

Ah, Michele, the reason I am sitting here writing – or trying to write – a letter of condolence to your family. Did I introduce Anna to you? I can't recall. She was obviously aware of how I treated her sister. When I was in the process of separating from my first wife – the Serbian, as Marie just called her in my dream – your wife took the Serbian's side. I believe that Anna often made nasty comments about me to you as you were writing letters to me. So many letters. A lifetime of letters.

Maybe Anna was right. Um, it was so long ago. I was in my late teens and early twenties. A romantic bohemian, carping on and on about the philistines all around me. Still, it was no excuse for my boorish behavior toward her sister, Marie.

It is strange, Michele, looking back, and not liking my former self, and then telling you about it. As if you didn't know all this.

And then there were the Winteler lads. Paul, who married my sister, Maja. She met him while she was studying at Aarau and boarding with the Wintelers, just as I had done. Maja and Paul lived in Italy, but between the wars the Italian fascists passed anti-Jewish laws and she left. Paul was sick and could not leave. She lived with me here in Princeton, planning to return. But she became ill and could not go back. Until she died, Paul wrote her letters, weekly. She missed him terribly. I forget what happened to him. Did we lose touch? Humm.

Ah Maja. She died here four years ago. When she was young she had a pretty face, not unlike her handsome brother. But later in life, like Elsa, she stopped carefully grooming herself, and as her hair turned white and got very long and frizzy, she and I looked alike. We were mistaken for twins, at times. Um, I miss Maja deeply, especially our evening times together, with me reading to her in bed. What did we read? She liked Cervantes's, *Don Quixote* – a long book, took us forever, uh, never finished it. She kept asking for it. I was not enamoured with it. Never knew what the fuss was about – a classic work? I see that today some writers are comparing me to the *Don*. They say that my quest for what I call my unified field theory is similar to the behavior of Don Quixote. They say that I am also just tilting at windmills. True, I may be on a quixotic quest, but I do not identify with Cervantes's fictional knight. Ug, why would I equate myself with such a self-delusional character? Oh, sure, some physicists believe that my search for a unified theory is a delusion – but, not I! Moreover, the *Don's* foolish and dim-witted behavior is appalling, and the excessive cruelty and violence in the book I find abhorrent too. I have a deep antipathy towards cruelty and hatred of all kinds. That's why I am against war. Simply put: war is murder. So, the book sat on the night table only for Maja's enjoyment. After she died I never opened it again. Now that I think about this comparison, I find it insulting. Me, as the *Don*? – rubbish!

Let's see: temperature, 41 degrees. Winds gusting to 15 miles per hour. The rain is getting heavier. I hope that, oy veh! Just remembered: the other Winteler son, Jost Junior. So painful to recall. I choke up, just thinking about it.

Sigh.

He went off to America as a cook on a merchant ship, or something like that. But after returning, he had a psychotic breakdown and shot and killed his mother and a brother-in-law – not Besso, thank God! – and then shot himself. What a despicable act. Pauline did not deserve that. Killed by her own son. Ah, what a terrible thing, such a tragedy for such a nurturing family. Humm, Marie, in my dream: said she never recovered from the heartbreak. Why did he snap?

Perhaps there was some mental illness in the family. Reminds me of the Serbian girl, my first wife. She who pushed Marie aside. Well, in truth, I did it. Mileva never met Marie.

Mileva Marić. She was the only girl in the advanced physics classes at the Poly. No one paid much attention to her, except me. The other guys did not find her attractive, but I found her – how should I say? – attracting. She was different: she was not bourgeois, like Marie – what I called incessantly philistine. Perhaps it was her Slavic qualities – dark, exotic, different. She had a limp. She went along with my bohemianism. We could talk physics. I found her sexy, a girl talking physics. Girls doing guy-things I often found erotic, like wielding a hammer, a girl with a hammer – exotic, erotic. It quickened my libido, as Freud would say. Ah yes, oh yes, Mileva and I had fun in bed.

At one point in the relationship she left the Poly and studied at Heidelberg University, since the relationship was getting too intense. We corresponded – about love, and physics. I said things such as, "I cannot wait to have you again, my all, my little beast, my street urchin, my little brat," and at the same time I reported on a book I was reading on the physics of gases by Boltzmann that I said was "magnificent." It really was; I used Boltzmann's work in some of the early papers I published. Mileva wrote me enthusiastically about a lecture she heard from a Professor Lenard at Heidelberg, in which he calculated the motions of colliding gas molecules. "Oh, it was really neat." Yes, she really said that. Okay, I know, I know, only a certain mind-type can get passionate about colliding gas molecules – well, she and I were both of *that* type.

Goodness, we were different from the others, and with the same weird and wonderful differences. Um, someday they may have a word for people like us.

When she returned to the Poly, the mutual passions for physics spilled over into the passions of the flesh. The phrase, "Oh, it was really neat" became a catchphrase in our lovemaking. "Oh, what you just did was really neat. Do it again!" From colliding molecules to colliding flesh.

We talked about really neat physics. We had really neat fun in bed. And, in a short time, we had a child – a child-out-of-wedlock, as they say. Not very neat, no, not very neat at all.

Well, few people knew about this, and few still know about this, even today. It is not in any of the biographies of me that have been published so far. Dukas, who knows, will probably try to hide this seedy-side of me from posterity, after I am gone. I don't care. Let historians find it and make a big deal about it someday.

Right now, the public views me as a sort of secular saint. Everything I say, they quote as if I were a fount of wisdom, a modern-day oracle. Geez, they exaggerate the importance of every little thing I do and present it as sensationally as possible. But like many saints, I too have my weaknesses. Yes, I can see the late-20th century headlines: EINSTEIN HAD ILLEGITIMATE CHILD.

Mileva gave birth to the child with her parents in Serbia. The baby was a girl, we named her Lieserl, and Mileva left her with her parents, as she returned to me in Zurich. I never saw my daughter. Never. What happened to her? SEARCH UNDERWAY FOR TRACES OF LIESERL. Late-20th century sleuths will be combing European vital statistics records to find what happened to our daughter. Something to keep the Einstein buffs occupied around the new millennium, eh?

Mileva bore the scars of the loss. I married her in January of 1903, a secular ceremony – but the fun was taken out of her. We had two children, both lads – Hans Albert in 1904 and Eduard in 1910, who we called Tete (or more affectionately, Tetel). She later had them baptized in the Eastern Orthodox Church. I did not object.

Family chores filled our lives in the first decade of the new century. My other life was filled with physics. Lots of physics. Important physics. I published papers that changed the course of science for the rest of the century, and probably into the new millennium. Relativity, quantum physics, atomism – science-things that intimidate the average folk. Esoteric. All done with little or no input from Mileva, despite the pre-marriage anticipation of our scientific collaboration – doing physics together. Um, it never happened.

Lieserl took the wind out of her enthusiasm for physics, so that she flunked her Poly exams and never got her advanced degree. A potential career in physics, very unusual for a woman at the time. But it was snuffed out by the birth of the child – at least that seems to be what happened. Yes, physics and love were intertwined for us during our student days. Yet, with science and sex so mutually buttressing each other, the demise of one led to the fall of the other. So, by the 1910s our relationship was strained, very strained.

Sigh.

At the time, I blamed it on hereditary factors. I still believe that heredity is important in human behavior. Freud believed in interpersonal and social factors. We corresponded once, on the topic of war. They published the exchange, since both of us were household names at the time. Freud and Einstein: two celebrities – and Jews too. Kept the anti-Semites on their toes. Um, I respect Freud as a writer. There is an engaging literary quality about his works. The linking of psychology to Greek mythology is brilliant – Oedipus, Narcissus, Thanatos, Eros. But the theory, I believe, is total nonsense. Ah, I was once almost cajoled into being psychoanalyzed. But I refused. Maybe I should have given it a go; to see what they think they might have found in my mind, sort of like having an astrologer read my horoscope. Oh, well.

Michele, we debated these things. Freud, psychoanalysis, what did you say? I cannot recall. Why in God's name am I talking with you about this?

Well, I attributed Mileva's behavior to heredity, since her sister, Zorka, had serious mental problems. Yes, she was diagnosed as being psychotic, and I concluded that it ran in the family.

Ah, yes, Besso, I remember. At the time, Anna blamed Mileva's behaviour on a combination of Lieserl and me. Your wife did not mince words; she was a strong outspoken woman, who was very frank in her feelings for me. At one point in our relationship, when she was taking Mileva's side, I vowed to cut your wife off from all correspondence, and perhaps even more. Um, but I didn't do it.

Mileva was depressive and continually irritable. She apparently never got over having given up her daughter. Our two lads did not fill the vacuum in her life that was left by the loss of Lieserl. Ug, how pitiful she was.

I dismissed Anna's argument, since she had it in for me because of how I treated her sister, Marie. And you both argued that Mileva's behavior could be explained by the tension and stress of the pending divorce, whereas I saw it as an inherited mental illness. But, you know,

Michele, with some maturity, I hope, and hindsight – I now think that maybe you and Anna were, well, at least partially right. Uh?

Well, I certainly was no model husband. My physics, almost always, came first. Well, in fact, it *always* came first. It consumed me. I made scant effort at helping with the lads when they were infants. Unless rocking a baby carriage while reading a book is being helpful.

So, Mileva and I grew further and further apart, and by the time our family moved to Germany I gave her the ultimatum that she must do all laundry, cooking, and housekeeping duties, but that there was to be no intimacy or any social interaction between us. Essentially, she was the hired-help, not a companion at all.

Oy, did I, in fact, have to be so nasty? Well, her brooding and un-communicativeness, along with some deep paranoia – I was at my wits end.

Sigh.

What is inherited, and what is not? I guess Anna Besso was right about some things. Giving up Lieserl certainly led to guilt and shame for Mileva. Indeed, Hans Albert– who now knows about his sister – remembers his mother's gloomy personality, and he once told me that she explained it to him as being based on something "very personal," as she put it to him. Um, it must have been Lieserl she was referring to, yes?

Ah, but other things I am sure *are* inherited. It is painful to ponder this, but, sigh, Tetel is now institutionalized in Switzerland, having been diagnosed in the early 1930s as schizophrenic. I believe it is part of the same internal rot that Mileva's sister, Zorka, got. And Tetel was so promising. He had so much going for him: a very good-looking young man. Gifted in music, literature, poetry. I was impressed with some of his poems. Do I have any? Um, was I much of a father? He had so much to offer the world. But, sadly, he is now languishing, getting fat, and chain smoking in the confines of a mental hospital. Um, mental hospital.

Oh, the year the family spent in Prague, with me teaching at the German University there, 1911-1912, the window of my office looking out onto what I thought was a park. But, when I noticed that only men walked around in the morning and only women in the afternoon, I inquired what, pray tell, was going on? So, I quickly was informed that the "park" was, in reality, the grounds of a mental institution, which explained everything. At the time, I was diligently working on my general relativity theory, and getting lost in long tensor-calculus equations of four-dimensional space-time. I once made a joke to a fellow physicist in Prague that I did not know who was crazier – me working on this seemingly impossible theory, or the inmates below seen from my window. Um, little did I know that in about a decade or so, my poor son, Tetel, would be a patient in a similar situation. Indeed, he was in the same institution where Zorka had been: Burghölzli, the well-known psychiatric hospital of the University of Zürich, located on "Burghölzli," a wooded area in southeastern Zürich. Ah, life has its slings and arrows.

Oy, I sound so hackneyed. As Americans would say – I am a real cornball father. Yet, I could not bear to be with Tetel when he was in one of his "states." We invariably got into a squabble if we spent too much time together, so I just drifted out of his life. I guess you could say we are now estranged. Mileva took care of him. I sent her money for support. It was not cheap – mental hospitals, living facilities. So, after Mileva died in 1948, I sold an apartment she owned in Zurich and used the money for continued support for Tetel. Oh, I surely never forgot him. How could I? I also sent money to Hans Albert. A total of tens of thousand of Swiss franks, as I recall.

Yet, both lads' attitudes toward me were poisoned by Mileva. They took her side. It is always that way – the father is the villain. Um, mothers are never wrong. Yet I did try to keep in touch with them through letters. Taking short vacations with them, when they would agree to go. I was not an awful father, I believe, was I?

Still, to be honest with myself, from today's vantage, I was partially the cause of the separation, I must admit. Especially, after we moved to Berlin in the summer of 1914. As we were living essentially independent lives in the 1910s, I became closer to my cousin, Elsa, who I knew since childhood. Elsa Löwenthal: divorced and living with her two daughters (Ilsa and Margot) in Berlin. I visited her on trips to Berlin for scientific meetings, and became increasingly attracted to her. Humm, in many ways she was the opposite of Mileva. Not an intellectual and with no interest in science, but with a very outgoing and sociable personality. Ordinary looking, she had a slightly chubby body; but with a catching and friendly smile, she could captivate people by making small talk. Yes, she was very good at this, a real charmer. Her home atmosphere was warm, cozy, and welcoming – what in Germany is called *gemütlichkeit.*

By the time our family moved to Berlin, a close bond had developed between Elsa and me. Yet, I could see that this bond was more than just cousin-to-cousin attraction. Mileva was aware of this and found it too uncomfortable to live with. Much too uncomfortable, and so she left Berlin, taking the boys with her, going back to Zurich. Humm, someone said I cried at the train station – cried like a baby. I don't remember. Ah, I was lonely.

So, I drifted closer to Elsa, psychologically and physically – moving into an apartment in her building. She gave me companionship, food, and space. Space, and especially time to work. Ah, space and time, the essence of my theory of relativity – a revolutionary theory of space and time, something I call space-time.

But, I missed my boys, very much. I was lonely, very lonely. Yet I did not miss Mileva. I was liberated.

Yes, um.

Michele, your wife Anna had strong feelings about Elsa. You and Anna were in the middle of the conflict among me, Elsa, and Mileva. Anna saw Elsa as the enemy, pursuing me, manipulating me. She saw this manipulation as a trait of the women in my family, such as my mother and sister. I know this from a letter Anna wrote to a common friend, who showed me the passage where she said that the Einstein women achieved what they wanted by "guile, kindness, threats, and pleadings." I remembered that quartet rather like I remember Hobbes's "solitary, poor, nasty, brutish, and short." Oh, that's a quintet; oh well, so much for the analogy. Anyway, I was livid with Anna at the time. But I'm not so sure I was right, now. Ah, revisiting these things in my mind is therapeutic, Michele. Well, that may not be the right word. But I do feel I am – how should I say? – re-living these feelings, and the distancing over time provides some insight into what was going on that I missed before, maybe. Are you surprised? Okay, Besso, I may have mellowed with age. I wish I could converse with Anna now. Yes, when I think about it, the Einstein women would sometimes use a combination of guile, kindness, threats, and pleadings to get what they wanted. Yes, they did.

Inevitably, I thought about divorcing Mileva. I thought about marrying Elsa. Maybe Elsa thought about it first. Yet Mileva still tried hanging on to me. I don't know what she wanted to keep, what she was trying to preserve. For me there was total emptiness in the marriage, a *vacuum* – a word, I think, I once used to describe what our relationship had come to. I promised her all the money from the Nobel Prize.

Of course, I had not yet received that Prize, but I was sure enough – cocky, smug – that the Prize was coming my way. And, of course, I did get it for the year 1921, and Mileva did get the cash. She used it to buy three houses in Zurich, two of which she rented out to live off the rental money, which she did for the rest of her life. Despite all this, she still was ceaselessly snivelling about money.

Sigh.

So, I finally got the Nobel Prize, Mileva got the money, and Elsa got, eventually, me.

     Elsa

          Elsa

               marriage

                       Ilsa

—How would you like to make our companionship permanent, Albertle?

—Elsa, why do you call me that South German, Yiddish-sounding name?

—I like it, don't you?

—Maybe I should give you a pet name? How about Tinef?

—Albertle! That's already the name of your sailboat. Your German-Yiddish concoction of a word.

—Since when did the socialite become a philologist?

—And how should I take that? You love your boat, so you love me? Or, is it a metaphor? What am I, since your boat keeps capsizing?

—Maybe it's an insult to my boat?

—How can that be, when Tinef means "a piece of junk"? Is that how you think of me?

—To me it is a term of endearment.

—Herr Professor Einstein, you can be so cruel some times.

—Sorry, but the idea of marriage leaves a bad taste in my mouth. Sure, I am comfortable here – but, frankly, too comfortable.

*—How can one be **too** comfortable? What are you, some kind of an ascetic?*

—Elsa, you are such a philistine!

—Ah ha! The bohemian world with Mileva still haunts you. Tell me, was it so pleasurable living in cramped apartments and dining on a meagre diet? Is that what you want to go back to? Albertle, you are smart in physics, but stupid in life.

—Of course, there is the biological problem.

—You mean, that we are cousins?

—Yes, cousins in two ways: our mothers were sisters, and our fathers were first cousins.

—But it is not against the law for us to marry. And we will not have any children.

—Maybe I should marry Ilsa?

—What! Ilsa, my daughter? Where did that come from?

—Well, for one: she can deliver another child, and she is not as close a relative. It does not have the same overtone of incest.

—But the gap in age between you and Ilsa would be an eyebrow raiser. Although, I guess, you would relish such a contrarian behavior.

—EINSTEIN, AGE FORTY, MARRIES TWENTY-TWO-YEAR-OLD COUSIN. Humm.

—At your age, do you want another child? Oh, perhaps a girl, since you and Mileva only had boys?

—Well, not really.

—*Not really? Not really what?*

—*Um, I, um, I am not really sure I want another child.*

—*So, why did you bring it up? What would people say?*

—*What do I care what people say? My oblivion to bourgeois conventions is a hallmark of my life. Indeed, I am thinking of not getting haircuts anymore.*

—*You socialist types have a penchant for flaying against the bourgeoisie for everything wrong with society. Bourgeois this and bourgeois that. Bitching about this very core of society that you are a member of. But, so be it: I will not try to mould you to my bourgeois ways. At least, not too much.*

—*The "not too much" is what scares me.*

—*I think I know what is truly going on here. It's about sex. Ilsa has been working for you as a secretary, and you have become attracted her. I hope, I pray, that nothing has been going on behind closed doors. Um, Albertle?*

—*Nothing, I swear.*

—*She is attractive, not chubby and dumpy, like me. I don't know what to say. You marrying Ilsa. Ilsa and Albertle ...*

—*Humm, Ilsa, Ilsa, Ilsa. So young, so attractive. My new wife, my lover. Let me mentally undress you. Yes, remove that, open that, and ....*

—Dukas! What do you want? Miss Dukas, why are you here? ***Shit, another erotic dream interrupted. Somnium interruptus? Ha.***

—Professor, you were dozing off again. Did I wake you from a dream? Sorry if I disturbed you. You were smiling in your sleep, again. What is it with you and that curious little smile? You know what Freud said about dreams.

—Freud said lots of things that were nonsense. But the dream stuff, well maybe there is something to that libido business and such.

—You are always dreaming Professor.

—Well, I sleep a lot, so that makes dreaming more accessible, no? Why, do you never dream?

—I seldom remember my dreams. But, now that I think about it, I do remember a dream of a few days ago. It was about you, in fact.

—Oh? Do tell.

—It took place in the present. You, Margot, and I were in this house, and burglars broke in and had us lined up against a wall. They were stealing our valuables, so they took Margot's watch and jewelry, then mine, but when they got to you there was nothing to steal. You were annoyed that you had nothing to give them, until you reached deep into a pocket and pulled out a dime. You were so pleased to hand over the dime, but the burglars, who missed the point, were not amused.

—What happened then, eh?

—I don't know. That's when I woke up.

—Just like me, when you get to the real intriguing or stimulating part of a dream, you wake up. Or, someone else wakes you up!

—I think it is your unconscious playing a cruel trick on you. Or, maybe it is an internal protection mechanism. Who needs dreams that are traumatic?

—True, but I was not thinking of traumatic events in dreams when I called them stimulating. I was thinking of, ah, oh well, glad to hear that you too dream, Miss Dukas. Hope to hear of more dreams. *I wonder if she has erotic dreams too?*

—We'll see, if I remember any more. In the meantime, we will just have to accept the fact that you are napping much more.

—It must be the aneurysm, slowly beckoning me to my grave.

—Don't say such things, Professor.

—I only wish I could complete my unified field theory before the damn pressure cooker inside me bursts. It's like a game. Get to the finish line before the bell rings: namely, the aorta pops! Working on this unified field problem for thirty years, even more, and still no definitive solution. Dukas, I advise you, put your money on the aneurysm bursting before I find the final equation.

—Professor, I am ignoring your macabre thoughts. Now, why did I enter this room in the first place? Oh, yes, the mail.

—I am still irritated that you censored my mail. Do you still do that?

—Only rarely. Mail from cranks and people trying to swindle you.

—Where is Tinef? I should get it out this summer.

—Professor, you are too old to go sailing. And the boat does not stay afloat properly.

—The capsizing is not the fault of Tinef.

—We'll see how things go this summer. Right now I am glad the rain stopped again, since the gardener can finish pruning the trees and bushes.

—Why not let them grow naturally, like, uh.

—What, like your hair!? No, at least something here we keep graciously trimmed.

—What is that package you have that came in the mail? I see you opened it already. And you did not throw it out, thankfully.

—I will ignore the latter remark. It is another long-playing record from Dr. Oppenheimer, who placed it on our porch. It is Mozart's *Requiem Mass*. After dinner, we will put it on the record player that the Institute gave you as a birthday present when you turned seventy.

—Oh, yes. These new 33 1/3 rpm high-fidelity records are a technological wonder. The sounds seem to reproduce a symphony orchestra right here in our room. How marvellous. But, the *Requiem*? Is J.R. trying to tell me something? You know, Mozart died before completing it. I sometimes think that he knew that he was, in fact, working on the *Requiem* for himself. Or, at least racing to get it done before he died. Just like me with my unified field theory. Of course, he never finished it. Did you know that it was finished by his friend Süssmayr, and there are some disputes as to how much of it – I believe the *Sanctus* and *Agnus Dei* – are by him and not by Mozart?

—You know your Catholic Mass, Professor.

—It helps if you go to Catholic school as a child. The school was close to our home and my parents sent me. Gave me a more catholic outlook, if you get my joke.

—Yes, Professor. I know the meaning of catholic, with a small c.

—Anyway, Mozart's last unfinished work reminds me of me. It is as if I died and Bruria Kaufman finished my unified field theory, and then she died and historians could not decide where my work ended and hers began. As you know, in December she and I finished the paper, "Relativistic Theory of the Non-symmetric Field," my latest attempt at a unified field theory, just being published. If I die soon, it will be my last publication in physics. Ah, it would be nice if she completed the whole theory. My first female collaborator. All those years, all those collaborators: Meyer, Infeld, Hoffmann, Bergmann, Bargmann – you called them "Berg & Barg" – Strauss, Pais, and now Kaufman. Many Jewish and many refugees from the idiotic fascism of Europe. How gratifying it is that Bruria is also an *Israeli* physicist. Um, that speaks for itself. And a woman too. I know I was never very open-minded when it came to appreciating woman's brains. Um, I was too enthralled with their bodies; well, at least, some of them. Looking back, I said some awfully stupid things about the intelligence of woman. I was very much trapped in the 19th century worldview I grew up in – a real stick-in-the-mud I was on this topic. I guess posterity will quote me on those dumb things, along with some of the smarter things I said. Oh, well. Such is another consequence of being famous. Humm, strange, isn't it? My first collaborator, you could say, was Mileva. We were physics buddies along with being lovers. For those few fleeting years, we were engrossed in physics together. Our love letters, especially mine, were a combination of mutual eroticism with each other and mutual rapture with physics. Humm, I had a very progressive attitude, thanks to Mileva. What happened? Yes, what happened? Something to think about. Mileva, you still haunt me in my old age.

—So, Professor. Um, Mozart and Süssmayr after dinner. In the meantime, I will have lunch prepared. Cabbage borsht and sausages. Okay?

—With tea. Yes.

—Of course. Black tea for you and Chamomile for Margot.

Michele, where was I? I was supposed to be writing a letter to your family, but I keep reminiscing, and falling asleep.

Elsa, marrying Elsa. I married her in June 1919, right after the divorce from Mileva went through; just a few months later. It broke a law, I believe.

Ah, 1919, a turning point in my life in another way – physics, of course. The Royal Society of London conducted the famous eclipse-of-the-sun experiment that proved my prediction from general relativity – that light from a star would be bent by a specific amount. Proved!! The light behaved – it bent just the right amount – just as I predicted. Ah, ha.

For God-knows-what reasons, journalists went into a frenzy and turned me into a new Newton – yeah, even beyond Sir Isaac, I was a light-unto-the-world of science. They called me a scientific revolutionary. Why the hullabaloo? Maybe it was just that the press needed something positive to write about after The Great War. Think about it: after four years of talk of death by bombs, mustard gas, and starvation. Enough! Europe was exhausted. So many lies. So many meaningless deaths. So much despair and anguish. I filled the vacuum of positive, optimistic news. Um, perhaps the fact that I was photogenic helped too. My mug shot was pasted in newspapers and magazines all over the world. Elsa and I were wined and dined in places we would never be admitted or even invited to – if we were just regular folk, especially *Jewish* folk. She loved the attention and the small talk.

At first it was all entertaining, but it quickly became tiresome and intrusive, having photographers flashing endless bulbs in my face – I called them "light monkeys." It all got to be boring: going to incessant dinners with long and mundane speeches. Well, it was not for me. Ah, I would amuse myself by jotting down my equations on the nonstop supply of napkins. I guess I was an intellectual snob. I was a boorish boor. A bored boorish boor. Ha.

But there was fun, too. Well maybe that's not the *right* word. Yes, I soon discovered that being famous has, you might say, benefits. Women are attracted to you as you never knew. It is real. I was flabbergasted. Who knew? I don't understand where it comes from, something about power, probably. At the time, however, the cause of this behavior was the last thing I fancied contemplating. Rather, I revelled in all this attention from women. Wealthy women, "looking for a good time" – as they liked to say. Ah, much better than tedious banquets and meaningless speeches. It was a fantasy come true – a fantasy too real not to indulge in. And so, indulge I did. Much to Elsa's chagrin.

She balked, she fretted, she yelled – but what were her options? She too revelled in the notoriety. She loved the limelight, the parties, the small talk – schmoozing with the upper crust of society. So, my dalliance behavior with other women was the price she had to pay. Anyway, it did not interfere with our interpersonal life, which was mainly platonic by then. Humm, what was she going to do? Was she going to divorce a husband again? To what end? At least, that was my assessment at the time: and so, I sowed my wild oats through much of the 1920s. Um, what did they call that decade? The roaring twenties? Ha, my whoring twenties.

Well, it became a problem when we needed to hire a secretary for me. Such a job was usually done by women, and it required close daily contact. After Ilsa, we went through many candidates, with Elsa rejecting any woman who appeared to be alluring to me. Miss Dukas? – well, she was a find, a real find. No flapper-girl in a short skirt was she. No way: a plain and proper young woman, who would not be a threat to Elsa, ever. Undeniably, Dukas has been hard-working and loyal, ever since. She was especially helpful when Elsa was sick and dying. Um, I must say that that Friday the 13th when Dukas got the job was *my* lucky day, and Elsa's too.

I don't think I have ever been very honest with myself about all this. Now is the time. What do you think, Michele, are you there?

I truly did not appreciate Elsa as much as I should have. She put up with a lot of shit from me. Oh, Elsa. Yes, you put up with a lot of, ah, my mother. Elsa, you were there for her, when my mother was dying of inoperative stomach cancer. Um, it was soon after we were married, and my mother wanted to move in with us in Berlin – to die, with us. I do not think I could have gone through this without your help. Elsa, you were an angel; newly married, and nursing my dying mother. Humm, she died in February 1920.

Sigh.

Elsa, when you died, I missed you. I realized how much I was attached to you, that I was not fully aware of. I wish I could say something to you now, to make you see how much you meant. But, since I don't believe in an afterlife, it's no use talking to the dead. Elsa, Mileva, Marie, to make amends. Amends? What the hell does that mean, after one is dead? Can I think of something, say, even funny, to remember you by? Oh, yes. There was that incident at a fancy dinner party. Your vanity kept you from wearing your reading glasses for seeing close objects when you were in public. So, on this occasion you dug into what you thought was the salad on our table, only to find out that it was a floral arrangement. Un-eatable flowers, that is. We had a good laugh for some time after that, didn't we? Um, rest in peace, Elsa. *Requiem aeternam dona eis, Domine.*

I look forward to listening to Mozart's *Requiem* this evening. Oh, Michele, I still have not drafted the letter to your family. Oy, am I not now speaking to the dead? Ah, where was I?

Elsa: marriage. Um, Hans Albert got married. Hans Albert, his wife, Freda. When Hans Albert told me that he wanted to marry Freda Knecht I was completely opposed. She was nine years older and very, very short. I thought she might have some heredity dwarfism. I told him he was marrying a dwarf! How could he? The children will be deformed. I also considered the possibility of mental illness in her family, and so I hired a detective. He found that Freda's mother had some problems with depression, but it was probably from a difficult childhood. Well, still, my concerns were fuelled by Mileva's sister Zorka being institutionalized around this time. So, I felt that Hans Albert's future with Freda would have hereditary problems on both sides of the family. Curiously, Mileva agreed with me on this.

Hans Albert was furious with me. He was in love. He was stubborn like his father, and so he married her. I then suggested that they have no children, but he (they?) did not listen to this, either. Yes, they had a child: a boy, Bernard, who grew up okay. Um, very much, a fine young lad. He visited me last summer. He is a better specimen of a man than his father or his grandfather. I believe he is a real *mensch*. In my will I am a leaving him my precious violin. Hope he appreciates it, someday. Hans Albert and Freda have a happy marriage, as far as I can see. All my consternation about their marriage was for naught. Ah, I was a fool. A real fool. A fool repeating my mother's foolish behavior. Mother and son: both fools about this.

Yes, humm, my mother's objection to Mileva. I recall it vividly, how many years ago? Mother burying her head in a pillow on a bed and crying uncontrollably, "You'll be sorry when she gets pregnant and ruins your life." Good Lord, she was right.

Mother wanted me to marry Marie. She knew the Winteler family, she corresponded with them. Pauline, shot dead by her own son. She could have been my mother-in-law. She too wanted me to marry her daughter. Yes, both Pauline's – my two mommies – they both wanted me to marry Marie. I disappointed them both – plus, of course, Marie! – because, in the end, I married the Serb.

Oh, my mother, by yelling and screaming, she just reinforced my determination to defy her and to marry the Orthodox Serb. Of course, I then repeated the parental act with Hans Albert. I was wrong to object to his marrying Freda. I was truly irrational. Yes, me – irrational. Who knew? So, Freda is a good woman, and a good woman for Hans Albert. He has had a successful career – despite carrying the burden of having the Einstein name. A better father and husband than I. Did I honestly say that? A far, far better husband and father, surely. It does not take hindsight to see that. Um, I am not ashamed to admit it, now.

Why was I such a poor father? Did I not have a good role model with my father? I seem to ruminate mostly about my mother, and sadly in the realm of complaining. Oh, those Einstein women. Why is my father in the background of my mind? He was an honest and cheerful man. But he was not as forceful as he should have been. (Rather like my lackadaisical friend Besso.) That is probably why he was not as successful a business-man as he (and my mother, especially) wished. This also manifested itself in his kowtowing to my mother; as when he supported her ranting about my relationship with Mileva. But I believe his heart was not in it – the ranting, that is. When Mileva and I finally decided to get married in 1902, my father was dying. I traveled to Milan to be at his bedside and I asked for his blessing for the marriage. Ah, he gave me his approval just before he died. How conventional of me, um. Of course, it was our last conver-sation, and I carry a deep emotional attachment to him from that day, even now. I am content having made that trip to Milan, despite the conventionality of this act. He died in October, 1902. How old was he? Let's see: Hermann Einstein, born in August, 1847, so he was only fifty-five. I've far outlived him.

Sigh.

Ah, yes, I still feel that same strong affection for him, as I recall all these things. Thankfully, I did ask for his blessing, however traditional it was.

Oh, Besso what a peculiar dream I had this week. After graduating from the Poly, I was desperately seeking a job. I wrote numerous letters to various scientists, one of whom was the famous scientist Wilhelm Ostwald. Despite my letter of introduction and a copy of my publication that cited his work, which I was sure would interest him, I never received a reply. In my dream, I was viewing my father writing a letter, with me peeking over his shoulder. He was, to my astonish-ment, writing to Ostwald too. He was pleading with him, praising my outstanding credentials and correctly saying that I was desperate for a job because I believed I was a burden to my family. I came out of the dream in a profound lament, feeling that I should have been a more devoted son. Although nothing came of my letter (and the one from my father; if, in fact, he wrote one), do you know that I later discovered that Ostwald was the first scientist to recommend me for the Nobel Prize? Ah, how unpredictable life can be – eh Michele?

So serendipitous, too. Which leads me to think: maybe my belief in the role of genetics in human behavior is an unconscious attempt to find some order beyond the randomness of life. It fits in with my philosophical belief in the basic predictability of nature in the physical sciences. This regularity of nature is the fundamental ground of classical physics, as the pre-quantum world is called. My objection to quantum theory is based upon the unpredictability of sub-atomic events, and because of this I believe the quantum theory is incomplete. Nature, I believe, is not random. There is determinism right down to the smallest level of reality. And none of this contradicts my relativity theory.

Nonetheless, when it comes to genetics, I suspect I have been wrong about the entire heredity thing. Indeed, it reeks of eugenics, a real pseudo-science popular early in this century: it was believed by too many otherwise intelligent politicians, physicians, and social theorists. Some of whom I met, such as George Bernard Shaw and Robert Millikan. Humm, I met Shaw in London around, I believe 1930, at a banquet for me. He gave the after-dinner speech. It was good and short: I did not fall asleep. He compared me to Napoleon and Newton, somehow, as I recall. Um, Millikan tried valiantly but unsuccessfully to get me to accept a post at Caltech in 1933, but I chose the new Institute in Princeton. Ah, yes, eugenics. Smart people believing dumb ideas. Indeed, the idea of sterilizing people, and treating them like rubbish? It previewed what the Nazis did. Ah, what was I thinking? I am ashamed to admit that I even thought about having Tetel castrated. Good God, this is a thought that still haunts me. It shows how much I too was persuaded by that eugenics nonsense. As Elsa would say: just because I know physics, does not mean I know everything. True: because physics is not everything.

But physics means a lot, a lot to me, anyway – it is my real love, more so than any woman. More so than anything – yes, any thing. I fell in love with physics about the time I fell in love with music. Humm, why do we *fall* in love? What does the act of falling have to do with it? We can fall into a hole. And then, for me, the act of falling is seen as an act involving gravity. What did I write one time, in jest? Falling in love is not the most stupid thing that we do – yet gravity is not responsible for it. Of course, I was thinking of people being attracted to people. Yet, we can use the falling image for other things. As I said, I fell in love with physics and I fell in love with music – and at about the same time.

Music. Oh, yes, the *Requiem* tonight, Mozart. Michele, did we not talk about the social role of music for us, or at least for me? It is difficult to articulate, but my exposure to serious music was a journey into another world, abstracted, even alienated from the everyday, and making me feel as if I were initiated into a sort of cult of like-minded people – knowing something esoteric that others did not, or could not, fathom. It made one feel distinctive, individual. Rather like a religion, but different somehow. Or, like knowing calculus – since so few do – but still different. As I said, it is not easy to explain. Did I explain it to you, Besso? Did you grasp my meaning? Did we even talk about this before? Michele, will you listen to the *Requiem* with me tonight?

Mozart, music, my love of music: a gift from my mother.

mother
        Mozart

David R. Topper

mother
Mozart

Music lessons. Practicing music. I fought this at a young age. Music lessons: torture for tots, cruelty toward children. But, by puberty, something happened, something snapped. I suddenly grew up: music was a way of touching the, um, the what? The unwordable? – I just invented a word. Ah, the 18th century called it the sublime? Something ungraspable, like the infinite. Oh, mother, you gave me my love of music. Mozart. About the same time, I was enamoured with geometry, and then calculus. Two loves: music and math, then physics. Symbols: flats & sharps – derivatives & square-roots – G clef & staff – $\sum$ & $\int$.

*It was a parallel love affair of math and music that filled in the mental hole in the mind of this early teenage lad – a hole that would otherwise be filled in with male bravado from the mundane quotidian world, like sports or emulating the odious militia – guns, swords, marching. The idiotic German fad of having a **schmusse**, a duelling scar on your face. Not for me. Humm, I believe that I never got into a fight with another lad after around the age of ten or eleven. No sports, certainly no contact sports, no physical horsing around. None of these male shenanigans. And no girls, the mania of male puberty. Yet, I do remember often waking up in the morning with my pyjama bottoms being wet and sticky, and then ...*

—Father, wake up! Come, come: it's one-o'clock. Lunch is prepared.

—Margot! Oh, I nodded off again, humm, no wet and sticky, uh.

—What on earth are you talking about?

—Oh, uh, the rain outside: walking in the grass, getting wet shoes, with grass sticking to the bottoms. ***Oy, what would I do now if my pants were wet and sticky? Ug.*** Ah, Margot, did I ever tell you a trick I pulled as a boy to get out of fighting?

—I know that you abhorred violence and fisticuffs as a young lad. But I don't recall anything about a trick.

42

—Well, I just remembered it. You see, I had poor dental hygiene, as they call it today – and my gums would bleed very easily. All I had to do was to pucker my month real hard like this … and blood would flow from my mouth. So, if a bullying lad grabbed me by my neck and twisted it, he would soon find blood running down his arm. Invariably, he would release me, lurching back in disgust or apologetically. It always worked; it kept me from getting hurt as a young lad.

—How interesting. The power of blood. Something to think about. Well, why I came up to see or wake you: lunch is almost prepared. Oh, by the way, I put an envelope on your desk that you may want to peruse someday. It contains some pictures that we found among your mother's belongings that Helen and I recently came across in storage. Anyway, come for lunch soon.

—All right. I'll be there in a few minutes or so. I am slightly groggy after this nap.

Margot. How long has she been living with me? Elsa's younger daughter. A contrast to her sensual sister, Ilsa. Dark hair, not very long, often parted near the top, and pulled back unattractively. A plain oval face, a long nose, and, what people called, sparkling blue eyes. Yes, but these eyes were often sad and forlorn. Seldom smiling. Um, I take that back. She and I have had many a good laugh. Belly laughs. Maybe I can bring these out of her, whereas others cannot. But she surely is shy. Indeed, when I first met her, she almost fainted. Humm, I believe she did, in fact, faint. Truly, she is the shyest person I ever met. Honestly, she would hide when guests came calling. Slinking under a table – truly, weird stuff.

But, a most gentle person. A real lover of animals and such. She nursed her sister, Ilsa, in Paris when she was dying. A good soul, a real *mensch*. I love her like a real daughter, since I never had a daughter. Oh, well, yes, there was Lieserl, ah. I suppose Margot is a sort of proxy daughter. Humm, never thought of that.

Well, I am glad Margot is living with me. A good companion. She is deeply drawn to art, especially sculpture. I have steadily encouraged her to pursue this art – a certainly solitary trade, and a good choice for a shy person. I am pleased with many of the works she has done. Working in clay, wood, wax, bronze, and, uh, terra-cotta, yes, that too. Mainly, small-scale sculptures; you can hold them in your hands. Um, she is now working on a wood carving of a grieving peasant woman. Modern, yet classical in some ways; classical being my choice in music and most of the arts. Order, symmetry, harmony, balance, Mozart, Spinoza, ah, yes, back to that.

Oh, Margot, we were surprised when that Marianoff fellow asked you to marry him. Later we knew why. A not very successful journalist, he kept prodding me to tell him personal details of my life. He eventually put our conversations together into a book: *Einstein: An Intimate Study of a Great Man,* by Dimitri Marianoff. It was published near the end of the last war. I am, at present, reading it again, trying to understand what there was about it that I found annoying when it came out. Humm, maybe it was just because I never very much cared for him.

I am sure he married Margot mainly to have private access to me. After the marriage, they lived at our home in Berlin with Elsa and I, and that speaks volume about the marriage. Good Lord, what kind of sex life could they have had with us around? Yet, Dimitri had constant access to me – and more, because he also worked for the Soviet Embassy in Berlin, and I wonder if he was also spying on me. We now know that the USSR had spies seemingly everywhere in the West. Well, after a short marriage – about seven years? – they divorced, which would be consistent with both of my hypotheses about his marriage to Margot. Oh, well. Margot eventually moved in with me, Dukas, and Maja. In my will, I am leaving this house on Mercer Street to her.

Before Maja died a few years ago, there were the four of us in this house. Yours truly and three women. I always like the company of woman. More so than men in some ways, um, in truth, in many ways. Women lack the coarseness, crudeness, boastfulness, conceit of so many men; locker-room behavior, which I find repulsive. I realized this sometime during my teenage years, as I was increasingly repulsed by many male lads, in contrast to what I saw among girls, or at least what I thought I saw from the outside, so-to-speak. There is something to say and emulate about femininity. Ah, yes.

Yet, on the other hand, I find the dependency of women ingratiating. What did I once say about this in a letter to Michele about Mileva? Something about the dependency of woman upon men, where they view us as kings, clinging to us, since they cannot stand on their own two feet. And if they do not have us as kings, they just fall to pieces. Ug, pretty strong stuff. I'm not sure I agree with that now, at least, not as strongly.

Humm, three women, alone with me. What did I call it? Ah, my henhouse. What did the neighbours think? My harem? Who cares. Just my style. Who knows? Someday in the future, after I am gone, someone may even speculate that Dukas and I had an affair. Oy, God forbid. It is one thing for the future to find out that I was not the saint they thought I was. But it is another thing to just make up fantasies.

Eh, Michele, what do you think? Do you remember that letter? What do you know about me that would surprise posterity? Would you tell me? Besso, would you tell the world?

Ah, I hear them calling me downstairs. What's for lunch? Borscht, sausage, and tea, I think. Um, the rain has slowed to just a drizzle.

2. Mid-afternoon

**"My relationship to the Jewish people has become my
strongest human bond ever since I became fully aware of
our precarious situation among the nations of the world."
— Einstein, 1952, to Abba Eban, Israeli ambassador**

Ah, back into, sinking into, my comfy striped chair. A blanket across
my knees and covering my legs. Relaxing as I stare out the window, onto
the grove of trees. Spring coming.

Daydreaming? I've been thinking about this lately, since I do it a lot.

Daydreaming is not a seamless, continuous, endlessly linked series of
thoughts, concrete thought. No, it is interspaced with periods – usually
relatively brief, but sometimes rather long – of what may be called
mental silences. Blanks. Voids. Breaks. Like silences in speech, there are
quiet intervals in thought, with no ideas in the forefront; yet they are a
real part of the mental world. Like brief moments of silence in a piece of
music, they are not nothing, but are part of the total pattern that constitutes the musical composition. Or, like blank spaces in a poem, where
they are part of the overall rhythm, interlinked with the words.
  Humm, one could apply the same visual pattern to a fictional text –
just letting the line or lines without a text represent moments of silence.
The greater the space, the longer the silence. Yes, nice idea: except, I do
not write fiction. Oh, well.

Albert, listen to what you just said, uh, well actually, what you
thought. Listen to the semantics: you used words and phrases such as

interspaced, not nothing, real, space. Think about it: your discussion of silence in thoughts, music, and poetry, sounds too similar to your concept of space in relativity to be an accident. Something to think about, eh?

Ah, Michele, you are so clever. Yes, for me space is not an empty nothing, but is a real, malleable, entity: an entity that causes gravity. Certainly, something to think about. Oh, Besso, we spent so many hours talking physics and more. You were my sounding board. It was a special experience for me. Prior to those years – except for the few student years with Mileva, and a couple of physics and philosophy buddies in Bern – I spent much, so much, of my intellectual life alone. For I am prone to long internal conversations with myself. Maybe that explains why I did not talk until I was about two-years-old – or vice versa? It's not the same without you. I am now reposing into my solitary world of speaking with myself, but I'm not lonely. You are still my sounding board for life. I enjoy these internal chats, my thoughts shared with you. Oh, burping up some sausage from lunch, aahh,

    aahh

          aahh

               aahh

                    aahh

Sausage, borscht, German food, mother's cooking, aroma at home, home in Germany, after school, coming home from school, chased by lads, lads calling me names, instigated by the teacher. Yes, Catholic school. Learning the Christian Bible. Not as raw as the Jewish Bible, which is full of lying, cheating, betrayal, adultery, murder – the sordid side of life. Yet, the story of Jesus dying from beatings, torture, and *crucifixion is not for the faint of heart, eh? Just think of Bach's interpretation in the **St. John Passion**. Well, not think of it, listen to it. Truly, I mean both to listen and to think. Recall the opening chorus: those thirty-six bars of throbbing bass lines, with the dissonance, and then the tension set up by the choir belting out those three chords of "Lord, ... Lord, ... Lord." The first one a minor chord – appropriately, for the subject matter – followed by a major chord, and last a diminished chord. The three chords setting up a deeper tension that pulses along with the bass line. What an opening to the two-hour masterpiece. Bach's use of dissonance was pushing boundaries for the time, as Mozart and Beethoven and others would do later. The passion of Jesus expressed through dissonance – the genius of Bach. I do not regret being exposed to the Christian story in Catholic school. Not at all. But: I didn't fancy the anti-Semitism.*

In reality, and fortunately, major clashes with my classmates were rare. They were serious, stern, humorless types. Intimidated by strict and authoritarian teachers. Already brainwashed into the militaristic frame of mind that would blossom later in the mayhem and madness of The Great War. Yes, a Great War: great for the munitions manufacturers, great for the chemical industry making mustard gas, great for the morticians selling coffins, making coffins out of wood and nails. Nails: Jesus was nailed to the cross, he died for our sins, and it was the Jews who killed him. Our dim-witted teacher brought that large nail to school, and holding it in front of the class declared that it was the nail that penetrated the body of Jesus, who was killed by the Jews. The nail: a relic. A relic of Jewish treachery.

*So, who was the only Jew in the class, and one of the smallest lads, as well? Little me, who had to run home from school that day. Run, run, Albert, the burden of the Jewish race is on your shoulders. Those dumb lads. Don't they know that the Romans killed Jesus? That Jesus was a Jew. Yeah, it is true; Jesus was a Jew, not a Christian – think about **that*** *my dumb German chums. I could teach you a thing or two. Yeah, but right now I need to run faster because you punks are trying to teach **me** a thing or two. Run, run ....*

—Ow, stop. Ow, stop.

—Take that you Jesus killer.

—Leave me alone, what could I have done. Why me, that was thousands of years ago. Don't you guys know anything? Ow, stop.

—Here, up against this tree. Give me a nail. Now you will see what it felt like for Jesus. Bam, bam, bam, goes the hammer. Yes, nail another Jew. Bam, bam ...

Bam, bam, bam ...

What? Where? Oh, it is the gardener hammering again in the basement. Oy, frankly, a nightmare. I must have dozed off. Oh, of course, my daily after-lunch nap. Humm, burping some of the German sausage.

Sigh.

German, Germany, dreaming of the nail incident. It is a trauma locked deep in the unconscious part of my mind. A ghost that remerges occasionally, haunting me, reminding me of my heritage. Grating at me: incessant, relentless, like the drizzle outside that just does not stop.

The gardener working in the basement. What is he making? Temperature 43-degrees, with gusts of wind up to 20 miles per hour. No walking outside for me today, it seems. So, little physical activity today. Yet, lots of mental action. Ah, yes, I am a man of action – mental action! I like to think, remember, dream, daydream.

Oh, yes, Besso, I know. I am trying to write a letter to your family. But daydreams keep creeping in. You understand, don't you? Michele, Michele?

We often went on long walks, Besso and I. It was, if I am recalling correctly, just such a long walk that resulted in the breakthrough in relativity theory about the concept of time – for which I thanked him, and only him, in my famous paper of 1905. His parents gave him a proper Italian name: Michel Angelo. Me, well, Albert. In truth, I was supposed to be named after a grandfather, Abraham. But my assimilated parents found it too Jewish-sounding, and settled for the less-Jewish, Albert. Just think, I was supposed to be Abraham Einstein. The famous scientist, Abraham Einstein. Would it have made a difference?

My parents were very ambivalent about their Judaism. Pushing it away, then pulling it back. Especially my mother. My father was quite anti-religious, I could say. As a youngster, I inherited this ambivalence. They sent me to Catholic school – because it was close-by – but they also gave me a Jewish education. Hebrew, Torah study, and such. In the long term, I developed a universalistic outlook on such things – ah, that's a good thing. But in the short term it drove them crazy, for I went into a very Orthodox religious period in my preteen years, probably in reaction to all this inconsistent religious education I was getting. I am sure they were sorry they sent me for Jewish instruction.

I was looking for something solid to stand on. Something to identify with. And so, I reprimanded them for not keeping kosher, for not keeping the Sabbath, for not saying their prayers – before meals, after meals, on waking up, before going to sleep, and more. Much more: I even made up my own prayers to God as I walked to and from school. It probably gave me a sense of security, being part of something larger – something beyond this pitiful earthly existence. Humm, I could consider it as my first experience of what I later called cosmic thinking, before I learned about real cosmology.

Fortunately, for them – and maybe me, too – this Orthodox phase did not last long, especially after I discovered science and mathematics. The catalyst was a Jewish medical student, Max Talmud, who my parents befriended in the Jewish tradition of giving a weekly meal to a poor Jew. Talmud: what a last name, the second greatest ancient text of Jewish literature. Although he later changed his name to Talmey, a less Jewish-sounding name, I suspect. I believe he did this after he moved to America. Oh, the pressure to assimilate into the Christian world at the time.

Max introduced me to the secular, scientific world; and I was bitten, for life. It started with a book he gave me on geometry. I was enamored by the fact that with just a few axioms and only the rules of logic, you could arrive at absolute truths. Mathematical theorems that were true everywhere and forever. I devoured that book, trying to prove the theorems myself, before seeing the proofs in the book. I recalled in my brief autobiography that I did this when I got to the famous theorem of Pythagoras about the sides of any right triangle. For sides a and b, with hypotenuse c, the relationship is true that $a^2 + b^2 = c^2$.

No, Albert. In your autobiography, you say that earlier you were introduced to Pythagoras's triangle by your uncle, and you solved it yourself using similar triangles. Take a look, it must be on a shelf nearby. Eh? I recently reread your autobiography, and it is still fresh in my head.

Oh, Michele, um. I believe you are right. I did prove it myself. But I did not appreciate the beauty, the logical beauty of geometry until reading that textbook, starting with axioms and such. It can't get any better than this, I thought. In my autobiography, I spoke of the textbook as "the holy geometry book" – a strange phrase. In contrast, *The Bible* and other religious texts were subjective and full of errors and untruths, as I came to believe. I went on to teach myself algebra and other math, so that around age sixteen I mastered calculus. That's why I had the letter from my math teacher in my pocket when I left Germany for Italy, after I dropped out of High School. Just in case, and it came in handy.

I also voraciously read popular books on science. Books on mechanics, electricity, magnetism, heat, optics, anything and everything I could find, especially on physics. All this left my previous passion over religious matters in the dust. More so: it was very much buried in the ground, never to be dug up again, I thought. I had found objectivity. Yes, the objectivity of the external world. How did I put this in the autobiography? Um, as I recall: Beyond the self there is this huge world that exists independently of human beings, and which stands before us like a great, eternal riddle, at least partially accessible to our inspection and thinking. Ah, yes: and I have never wavered from that intellectual framework.

Alas: all this happened right before my intended Bar Mitzvah, which consequently never took place. Maybe that's why I later called the math book "holy," since it replaced a different holy book. Humm.

Ah Michelle, why am I avoiding the letter to your family? Only a letter. Michele, you were my closest friend in those halcyon days at the turn of the century. Along with Marcel Grossmann, Maurice Solovine, and Conrad Habicht, my physics and philosophy buddies. My closest friends – excluding Mileva – were almost all Jews. This must mean something. Maybe my Jewish identity was not as buried as I thought.

I certainly avoided any overt relationship with any formal aspect of Judaism. I led an entirely secular life with my Serbian

Orthodox wife, right through the first decade of the 20th century. I published paper after paper on physics. I worked in the patent office in Bern. I got professorial positions at universities: first, the University of Zurich, where I obtained my PhD; then at the German University of Prague. Humm,

Prague
1911-1912
Czechs & Germans & Slovaks
ethnic prejudice rampant

—*Mileva? Are we in Prague?*

—*Yes, Albert. And it is awful. I hate it. Let's go home.*

—*It has only been six months. But I agree with you. The water is almost undrinkable. The educational system is very poor, and Hans Albert is required to attend Catholic school, with much brainwashing. The bureaucracy at the university is Byzantine. It is all endless ink-shitting. Moreover, the Germans are snobs, looking down on the Czechs. The Czechs hate the Slovaks. This narrow-minded ethnic hatred and tension I find offensive and uncomfortable. And they all hate the Jews. No wonder I have begun thinking seriously about Zionism as a viable option. On this entire planet, somewhere there must be a little patch of earth on which my ethnic comrades will not be considered aliens.*

—*And as a Serb I am uncomfortable here among the Germans. The ethnic bigotry is more than offensive – when I have to endure anti-Slavic jokes. Albert, I've made no friends.*

—*I have, however, made much progress in my work in physics. Plus, there is that group of unworldly-like intellectual Jews that we have met, who seem to have come out of the Middle Ages. I do enjoy their company, most of the time. They certainly are smart, and I have benefited from the discussions about Spinoza, my hero – my Jewish hero. I have had little time to ruminate on Spinoza since my days with Solovine, about a decade ago, when we read the* **Ethics***. I enjoy reading and discussing this treasured but difficult book again. Also, I have been drawn to the group's speculation about Zionism as a way for European Jews to deal with the dreadful anti-Semitism that seems to be ubiquitous and never-ending. Very much something to think about, very seriously. But the group's flirtation with various versions of Jewish mysticism I am not attracted too, not at all. In the end, we will probably leave here after just one year.*

—I would say, Albert, that you have rekindled your Jewish identity since being a member of this group. I only wish you would rekindle your interest in me too. You know, I crave attention and love. Some, uh, intimacy?

—These Jews are so intelligent and explorative – what's not to like about them, especially that Kafka fellow? Franz has not yet published anything, but I suspect that when he does he will make a big splash on the literary scene. And, yes, I too hope we can go back to Zurich, as soon as possible.

—Albert, you are ignoring my pleading. Um, maybe if I changed into something more comfortable, and displayed some of the risqué movements you always liked ..., like this, ... and this, ... and

Oh, I dozed off again. Whew, the wind is strong, and the rain beating on my window, it woke me up. Such gusts of wind.

Sigh.

Well, yes, the family did go back to Zurich, since I got a job at – of all places! – the Poly, where I had *not* been one of the outstanding students. Um, that puts it mildly. How ironic, or is it making amends – on both sides? There's that phrase: making amends, again. Anyway, Kafka certainly did create a literary sensation. His work continues as being almost prophetic, especially as we progress further into this century – although the word "progress" no longer rings true, anymore.

Albert, you are ignoring Mileva's attempt at tempting you into bed. Unlike your erotic dreams about Marie and Ilsa, you are not upset at this one being interrupted.

I know, Michele, you are supposed to be my center of thought. Condolences to your sister and son. How to start?

Zurich did not last long. Berlin beckoned, with an offer (as they say) that I could not refuse – although I hesitated, very much, since it meant returning to the country that I renounced at age sixteen. At the same time, it was a job at the world's center of physics, and with no teaching duties; it was just too tempting. So, I went to Berlin and, as I wrote somewhere, I discovered my Jewishness through the endemic anti-Semitism for the first time. Yet, this was not quite true, because my Prague sojourn initiated a rekindling of that heritage. Of course, I was exposed to anti-Semitism before. But in Berlin it was, well, more – how to say? – immersed.

Indeed, I took up the plight of Eastern European Jews. It was a problem that I was particularly drawn to. In the late-19th century there were waves of Jews fleeing pogroms in Russia, going into Poland and some further into Germany. During the Great War, they were recruited for doing war work while living in poor conditions. After the war, those who did not move to America or Palestine were consider parasites and vermin by the Germans. Even the assimilated Jews generally avoided these Ghetto-living, Yiddish-speaking, skull-cap wearing, co-religious folk, who took simple jobs, such as peddling goods. But I could not stand idly by and impartially watch this discrimination of a minority. I wrote and lectured in support of these Eastern Jews. I pointed out that the Germans were accused by the enemy of acting like barbarians during the war, and that their treatment of the Jews simply reinforced that stereotype. I also argued that these Jewish peddlers were not hordes of beggars, but were a wealth of fine human talent of productive energy – and, which we now know, was true. Just look today at the contributions of Jews in the countries in which they were able to flourish; at least, those who survived the German extermination. At the time, I arranged for special lectures for Eastern Jewish students at the University, for those not regularly admitted. All this was part of my reengagement with my Jewish identity.

Another part of this: I increasingly saw a role for Zionism. So much so that I accepted a request to tour America in the spring of 1921 in support of Zionism, especially to raise funds for the creation of a Hebrew University in Jerusalem. Quickly this became a pet project of mine. My support of Zionism, then and even now, was more in terms of Israel as a cultural entity than as a nation-state. Nonetheless, I have, finally, reconciled my ambivalence: today I accept Israeli nationalism as unique, after the war of independence following the genocide during the last war.

In the 1920s, however, my focus was on a Hebrew University. I was chaperoned in America by the chemist, Chaim Weizmann, president of the Zionist movement and later the first president of the state of Israel. I knew I was being used to attract potential donors – a prize-winning ox, I called myself – but I accepted that role. I wrote at the time that I was very much doing whatever I could for the brothers of my race who are treated so badly everywhere. And it worked – yes, potential donors came up with money. Although we did not raise as much cash as Weizmann hoped, yet the trip was important in my life for even further acquainting me with my Jewish identity. I was impressed with how American Jews had a strong Jewish identity, much more than the assimilated European German-Jews I knew, such as my parents. The Americans also were not as defensive about their Judaism; it was a more relaxed and assertive identity than in Europe. It was a real revelation for me. Perhaps this prepared me for later accepting the move to America, after the rise of Hitler.

I also discovered what a celebrity was. Those Americans certainly know how to treat a guy. Crowds everywhere, gawking at me. Endless photographers wasting lots and lots of flashbulbs and film. How many pictures did they need?

All was not fundraising, however. There was an ulterior motive for my acceptance of the trip to America. I was proselytizing my relativity theory, especially at visits to universities in New York, Boston, Chicago, elsewhere, sometimes even lecturing on my ideas; I wanted to expose my theory to a wide range of physicists. Indeed, at Princeton University, I gave five lectures that were published as the book *The Meaning of Relativity*; in fact, my recent article in my quest for the unified field theory is to be published as an appendix to the latest edition of that same book. Little did I know at the time that in a dozen years I would commence the rest of my life in the town of Princeton, New Jersey, not far from the University. Life is funny that way. Of course, funny is not the appropriate word for what happened.

Sigh.

Besso, I know, the letter to your family. I'll be getting to it.

Besso, Besso, BESSO, ESSO, ESSO GAS, gas, poison gas, mustard gas, The Great War, Fritz, Haber, Fritz Haber. Yes, a tragic story. Or maybe better said: a wretched story of a Jewish life in 20th century Germany.

Haber, powerful job, director of the Institute for Chemistry in Berlin, and the major mover and shaker in getting me the job offer for my relocation from Zurich to Berlin in the summer of 1914. We met at a scientific conference a few years before and struck up a close friendship. Both almost the same height, but Haber was mainly bald, with a trimmed moustache. Wore round rimless glasses, and was ever impeccably dressed in a neatly pressed three-piece suit. In Berlin, Mileva and I became close friends with Fritz and his wife, Clara. He was ten years older than I. Jewish too, but very different in many ways. He was a secular Jew, as I, but he converted to Lutheranism in his mid-20s in order to fit into German society, hoping fully to eliminate the otherwise social blocks to Jews along the roads to potential success. Haber also was a strong nationalist, a real German patriot, whereas I was always vehemently repelled by all forms of nationalism. Excessive nationalism is like a disease, spreading throughout society. In fact, jingoistic nonsense. And then there was the German male ritual of dueling. There are no dueling scars on my face. Also, excessive beer drinking. Me? The teetotaler. I was out of sync with so many Germanic customs – behaviors that I found to be crass. Ah, where am I going?

Oh, Haber. Yes. Ah, Nobel Prize in Chemistry (1918?), for synthesizing ammonia from nitrogen and hydrogen, a discovery that revolutionized the production of fertilizer, making high yields in agriculture possible here and throughout the world. He was a real hero for alleviating starvation. Yet, there was another spinoff: the application to make explosives from the same process. Fertilizer used to make explosives, bombs, how peculiar. This he explored further during the war, producing mustard gas. He became the chief scientist for the war effort. Got medals for his work, a chest-full of metals, and accolades – a real war hero.

But this dark side had its consequences. His wife, Clara, could not live with the realization of so many deaths from this chemistry: his chemistry, her husband's chemistry. She took her husband's pistol and shot herself. The honors, the medals at the end of the war, were a bitter-sweet reward. So many died in the Great War. Clara was a war casualty.

But more, much more. Haber's distinguished war record, his conversion to Christianity, his Nobel Prize, his hard work for Germany in science and industry: it all, every single bit of it, it *all* came to naught when Hitler came to power. They did not kill Haber directly, although they probably would have, eventually. As Jews and others deemed hostile to the Nazis ideology lost their jobs, Haber foresaw his fate and he fled the country. The Nazis entirely erased Haber's record of achievement from German history books, as if he *never even existed*. He was a broken man, and died of a heart attack in Switzerland, a year later.

But the fallout was not complete. Haber's Institute went on to develop, as a pesticide, Zyklon B, which in the 1940s was used in the gas chambers to kill some of Haber's friends and relatives, along with millions of others. His son, Hermann, found refuge in America, but committed suicide, as his mother had, in the late 1940s. Shortly thereafter, Hermann's oldest daughter did the same. Does it never end?

Tragic Fritz. Poor Clara. She too was a convert from Judaism. Were they naïve? Could anyone have foreseen what would transpire?

gas chambers
genocide
Goethe
gemütlichkeit

—*Fritz, how is your work going?*
—*I assume better than yours, Albert. No unified field theory yet?*
—*Still plugging away. Some day, maybe, a breakthrough.*
—*We are finding some further important applications of these fertilizers for explosives and pesticides.*
—*Do you not see any sinister side to this work?*

—Albert, you should know, scientific work is all for the good of mankind.

—But, frankly, it isn't that way, Fritz. I believe that the benevolence of all mankind should always be at forefront of the scientist's mind as he works at his tasks – even when pondering his diagrams and manipulating his equations – because he never knows what the applications may be.

—Well, possibly, yet we do not always have control over what others may do with our discoveries. Of course, I did control the applications of mine.

—I hate to bring this up, but Mileva told me that Clara had very strong misgivings about your work. I wish I would have warned you.

—Albert, it probably would have made no difference. What does a woman know about such masculine work? It was an unavoidable tragedy.

—Fritz, do you have any misgiving about being such a high-profile Jew?

—As you know, although most of my friends are Jewish, I am officially a Christian and immune to the anti-Semitism of the right-wing in this country. As well, I think that this present right-wing agitation is just a temporary aberration that will pass, because there is a democratic core in the German nation. A country that gave us Goethe and gemütlichkeit, has its limits of intolerance, I should think. Albert, you too, I believe, have said the same.

—Yes, I was quoted as saying that all this will blow over, as most Germans will come to their senses. But I hope you, uh we, are not naïve. Ever since I moved back to Germany, as an adult, I have been sadly aware of the endemic anti-Semitism in this country.

—It is ever-present, just below the surface of society, and I think, hope, that it will remain there.

—I wish it would go away, so Jews could live, not only in peace, but without any apprehension. I am quite sure that many of my difficulties in getting jobs after my degree were due to my Jewish identity.

—Which reminds me, Albert, you never told me why you never converted.

—We never talked about it. It never came up, despite our close friendship. Indeed, our friendship is rather strange, for we are opposite in many ways. You, a nationalist. Me, an internationalist. You, proper, with social graces. Me, a contrarian, with shoddy dress. You, cheering on The Great War. Me, signing an Anti-War document. And so forth.

—So, why no conversion, just to be different from me in another way?

—Frankly, Fritz, I am quite sure I never ever even considered the option. I was, I admit, ambivalent about my Jewish roots many times in life. But the idea of conversion would have been anathema to my negative attitude toward authority and my inherent contrarianism. It would mean that I would believe in something I find impossible. Moreover, ever since my trip to America to raise funds for a Hebrew University in Jerusalem, and my trip to Palestine seeing Jewish workers building and farming and reviving a culture on this ancient soil – well, I find I am more and more identifying with my Jewish roots. The more I think about the precarious situation of our people among the nations of the world, the more I bond more closely to the Jewish people. This bonding, for me, replaces the idea of a Teutonic folk tilling the soil of Germany, the "soil and blood movement," an idea that is so much in vogue today, going under the pseudo-scientific label of Aryanism. You may have heard me speak often of my Jewish friends as part of the "tribe." This tribalism is not the Aryan version found in the dark forests of Germany, or expressed in the music of Wagner.

—I admit, Albert, I find this Aryan mumbo-jumbo scary. But I still hope my conversion makes me immune to any significant social ostracism.

—I hate to say this, Fritz, but I recall saying somewhere that baptized Jews of past and present are "pathetic creatures,"

    pathetic creatures
            pathetic creatures
                    pathetic creatures

Pathetic. Oh, a heavy gust of wind rattled my window, again, and woke me up.

Sigh.

Yes, pathetic. So many Jews converted. What did I read about this? Even before modern times, there were the *Marranos* in Spain and Portugal who, despite becoming seemingly devote Christians, nonetheless were persecuted and even tortured and executed during the Catholic Inquisition; and the rest later were expelled in 1492. Columbus went west and the Jews went east, the latter scattering again across Europe wherever they would be accepted, or perhaps better said, be tolerated – such as Spinoza's ancestors who fled the persecution and settled in Amsterdam. How interesting that the word *Marrano* in Spanish means pig, a common derogatory argot used by the Nazis for us. The collective memory of the martyrdom of the *Marranos* haunted Spinoza's Jewish community in Holland in the 17th century, just as the slaughter of the Jews of Europe will haunt the next generation of Jews today – and after, I am sure.

Humm, back to the Habers. I once read that during the last century there were about 2000 conversions a year in Europe, and this may be continuing and amplifying in this century. There were many famous members of the tribe. Heine, the beloved poet, and Kronecker, the important mathematician. And musicians, especially Mendelssohn, and later Mahler, who did it because otherwise he could not get the director-ship of the Vienna State Opera. Which brings up the incessant issue of the possible influence of Jewish music on these two composers. I am not familiar enough with these modern composers to see this, but it does bring to mind my nominal exposure to Jewish ceremonial music. Yes, I fondly recall sitting through a Jewish service in California and being particularly moved by a version of the *Shalom Aleichem*. There was something almost Middle Eastern about the harmony that tapped into my inner space: it also felt a bit Japanese in its dissonance. The same is true for my experience with the *Kol Nidre* prayer at *Yom Kippur*. I am there-fore pleased that J.R. is trying to nudge my musical tastes into the present century by introducing me to elements of Mahler.

Why Mahler? I thought no one plays his works, but J.R. said there seems to be revival of this otherwise obscure composer. I must say that the recording of Mahler's *Rückert-Lieder* that he gave me for my birth-day is very enchanting. Based on the poems of Friedrich Rüchert, the songs are sung by the contralto Kathleen Ferrier with Bruno Walter conducting. I especially like the song about world-weariness and death; the haunting melody of the oboe and the melancholy poem are quite beautiful. I am so enthralled that I have been trying to memorize the entire poem, ah, but my memory is not very sharp anymore. Um, "I have become weary of the world, the world thinks I am dead / I live alone in my heaven, in my love, in my song." Ah, that's all I can recall. I need to look at the phonograph record's back-notes again. Um, what makes the recording even more poignant is that Kathleen Ferrier was dying of breast cancer at the time of the recording a few years ago, and she died the following year in her early forties. Here I am at seventy-six and world weary. I believe J.R. thought I would identify with the poem – and I do.

Perhaps *my* song is the search for a unified field theory. It's a better analogy than silly Don Quixote.

Ah, yes: "I have become weary of the world, the world thinks I am dead / I live alone in my heaven, in my love, in my song."

Mahler's melody, in my head, so lovely, I should play the record again tonight. So much of his music, J.R. told me, is about homeless wandering, no doubt the theme of the wandering Jew. His Christian conversion was merely to open doors in the music climate of Vienna that otherwise were barred to him. Of course, all European musicians were exposed to the huge repertoire of Christian music, which was experienced by Jews as outsiders. That was surely a substantial magnet to getting closer to the music. But, still, conversion was a large leap.

Sigh.

And so, what was I thinking? Oh, yes, the contrast between American and German Jews. (In fact, I recall that Mahler was not German, but Czech or Bohemian. Humm.) The Americans have a confident sense of self-identity; who they are and are not. The Germans are too self-conscious, fretting that their Jewish identity will conflict with their German nationalism. They could learn to be more comfortable with this, as the Americans are. Ah well. Rest in peace, Fritz. And Clara. Clara and Fritz. Fritz and Clara.

Fritz 'n Clara
> Pizzicato
>> *music*
>>> *recital*

A recital concert at the Princeton music school. Avant-garde music, Margot took me: she wanted to go but was apprehensive about going alone, timid in public. We stayed for two recitals. The first was a quartet. I love the sound of chamber music, which is the format in which I have played many times. My many travels with Elsa across the seas, when I took my violin. It was easy to find others looking for musicians to play with on the ships. Trios, quartets, quintets, small groups – so much music on those often-long ocean voyages. So much pleasure making beautiful music.

But the concert at Princeton with Margot was, well, something else. The sounds coming from the quartet were repetitious to the Nth degrees. Cycle of notes, with small variations of key or tonality. I closed my eyes and used the time to contemplate some mathematical problems with my unified field theory that I was working on at the time. It seemed to work; the repeating notes put me into a state that abstracted me out of the material world. Oh, if only I could have made a great breakthrough that night; I would have been eternally grateful to that composer. In fact, he probably would have been immortalized. And, of course, psychologists would study the music looking for clues to how the notes stimulated the cells in my brain, etc. But no such thing happened; there was no mathematical inspiration. I am still plugging away at the theory.

When I came back to this world, the piece was over and Margot was nudging me to wake up, thinking I had dozed off. The second recital began with what I thought was a solo piano piece. It consisted of one man, seated on a swivel stool with wheels, at the piano. He was quite skilled at arpeggios and making large leaps across the keys. He must have practiced endlessly. But I quickly realized that there was another element to the piece. As it progressed, he switched to hitting what seemed to be a random series of notes up and down the keyboard, and further, he would often reach into the piano and pluck the strings (pizzicato) – all the while he moved the swivel stool with his body and feet. But, to my dismay, there emanated from the stool itself various squeaks and squeals to accompany the piano notes. When I realized that the sounds from the stool were a purposeful part of the recital, that the stool was a sort of accompanying musical instrument – well, I could not help myself and started laughing out loud. My boorish behavior at this serious music concert was not well received by some members of the audience, who turned around to give me what Americans call "a dirty look." Margot was uncomfortable at all this commotion and grabbed my hand indicating that we were leaving the so-called concert, right now, immediately. I did not resist.

—We are out of here.

—Okay, Margot, okay, I get the message.

—I am mortified.

*—Oh, Margot, why do you care what other people think? And, anyway, when they saw it was **me**, they smiled. Remember, I am a sort of secular saint, who can do no wrong for the masses.*

*—I am still mortified. And at a **classical** music concert.*

—Well, classical music is much too uptight about social manners and the etiquette thing. Even though I am no fan of jazz music, look what background noise jazz musicians must put up with when they are playing, often with glasses and plates rattling and clinking, and people chatting and laughing. It should be a lesson to the classical snobs. I became aware of this during one of the three visits to California with your mother. We were in a place called Palm Springs at an estate of a movie producer, and I played music with two young jazz musicians. They taught me a lot. Oh, I just had a thought; maybe that was what the stool's squeaks and squeals were all about – integrating background noise into the music.

—That is quite a rationale for the noisy chair, Father. But I do agree that the concert was not much in terms of what I call serious music. It

pushed the boundary much too far. But I am afraid that this is the wave of the future.

—Maybe someday someone will write music about me. Say an Opera about my life. Considering my status in this century, I would not be surprised.

—And it will probably be written in the avant-garde style of this concert with the tedious repeating cycles of melody. Um, that would be a laugh.

—Ha, yes. Margot, since when did you get so funny?

—Well, anyway, at least in the solo piano concert, the man displayed himself as a splendid pianist.

—What, he displayed his splendid penis? Did he expose himself? Did I sleep through it?

—Father! Not again! Did you forget that mother was disgusted with your scatological remarks, and for a time she cured you of this bad habit? Let's just be quiet as we walk home.

—Okay. But we need to pick up our pace. The rain is coming down again, with strong winds blowing from the north.

Ah, rattling the window, again. What a wind! Oh, what a strange dream. Dreaming of my own narration of the past. Why? Is it true? Did it happen? The concert? What does it mean?

Albert, how slick. If you had to type this dream of a narrative, you need put it into a different font. Yes?

No, Michele. You know I cannot type. Dukas does all the typing for me. Always has. But, yes, she could put it into another font, of course.

Um, I see I mentioned jazz music. I am so much steeped in European classical music that I seldom open myself to other expressions. Well, there was my introduction to eastern music during our tour of the Far East in the early 1920s. I did find Japanese music interesting from a formal and structural viewpoint, but the sound was jarring and very grating to my ears. I was, however, quite enamoured with Japanese art and calligraphy; indeed, they are often blended together in the same work. In many of the ink drawings there is a lovely tension between the free, almost improvised, draftsmanship and the strict formal structure to the content itself. As well, the simplicity of it all appealed to my well-known partiality to the principle of parsimony. I am instantly attracted to anything exuding what I see as having some semblance of what I believe today is called minimalism; at least, that is what Margot calls it. It is true too of Japanese interior design: the severity of it all and the almost asceticism of expression is a far cry from the cluttered Victorian sur-roundings of our Berlin apartment. And which, sadly, Elsa had shipped to Princeton and now fills my home. So much for simplicity.

Despite my taking a liking to the warmth and graciousness of Japa-nese culture, I also took notice of a dark undercurrent expressed in their worship of ancestors and the similar cult of the emperor. I am instantly repelled by anything reeking of unchecked authoritative power. So, I was uncomfortable with the militarism and chauvinism of it all. Of course, I could not foresee how far this would go in a decade or so. Ah, it troubles me to realize that the excessive war crimes of the Japanese army in China were a gloomy and gruesome prelude to the genocide of the Nazis.

Ug, I always seem to come back to the Nazis. No matter how genteel and civilized a culture may be, it is no shelter from a possible descent into barbarism, it seems.

Sigh.

Where was I? Oh, yes, music, European music. I am unashamedly partial to Western harmony. The diatonic scale, with the interplay between the tonic, dominant, and subdominant: I believe it is a gift to the world. There is nothing like it elsewhere – although I have been told that the perfect fifth and such are, indeed, within Eastern music; well, maybe, but my ear cannot hear it. Drowned out by the dissonance I hear.

Importantly, I see a correspondence between the diatonic scale and European Renaissance art, with the breathtaking deep spaces and glorious details in the oil paintings. Yes, the whole linear perspective thing of the 15th and 16th centuries in Italy and Flanders was unique to history, so Margot and Erwin tell me; only to be followed by another singular event – the Scientific Revolution of the 17th and 18th centuries.

Erwin?

Yes, Besso. Erwin. Uh, Erwin Panofsky, the art historian at the Institute, a friend of mine, told me about the scientific connection. He said he was going to write about this. Oh, yes, he too was a refugee from Nazi Germany in the 1930s.

Ah, but jazz was what I was thinking about. The Nazis lumped it in with all of what they called "degenerate art." Jazz, in particular, was deemed Judeo-Negroid music. So, we Jews were amalgamated with the black race. Considering my outspoken criticism of the social situation of colored people in this country, I would deem the association a compliment by Herr Hitler and his cultural henchmen. In fact, I would go so far as to say that the wonderful songs and chants of the Negros are the finest contribution to the realm of art which America has given to the world. Yes, indeed.

Oh, what fools those Nazis were, and in control of a country with long history of, ah, what more can I say about this stupidity. Indeed, the

Germans have a wretched history, going back to the late Antiquity – the Romans called them barbarians. And they are still messed up, and almost impossible to redeem. During the last war, I once said that I hoped, with God's help, the Germans might just kill each other off. That I went so far as to appeal to help from the Lord, shows how desperate I felt. For me to say this – I, who does not believe in a God who interferes or meddles in any way with human matters. Well, humm, God's help. Yes, God's help.

Sigh.

Why do I keep recalling it, and dwelling on it? Though, think about it: who were the Nazis to deem something *degenerate*? Gas chambers for committing mass murder, genocide – now that was a sign of degeneracy. Yes, I truly should open myself to jazz music. Maybe, someday. Humm.

Ah, the rain and wind have subsided. I gaze out at the damp-green garden through Elsa's bay window. Ah Elsa. Sadly, not long after she finished remodeling this house, she got word that Ilsa was deathly sick in Paris. She traveled there – I stayed home, there was still a price for my head-on-a-platter in Europe – and she was with her daughter when Ilsa died of tuberculosis. It broke Elsa's spirit. She was never the same. Even the peace and quiet of our abode here in Princeton could not alleviate her disquiet. She died on me in 1936. When was it? December something. At times, I believe, I miss you, Elsa. Ah, did I actually think that thought?

Well, the tranquility of this garden was in dramatic contrast to the chaos we left in Berlin. How to live with young men with swastika armbands roaming the streets, looking for trouble – no, making trouble? Princeton was a sleepy town in comparison. I am privileged by fate to live here; as if on an island, isolated from the chaotic voices of human strife, especially in Europe. I am almost ashamed to be living in such peace. Yes, I love my, er, *our* garden behind our home. In the far back edge of the garden we made a flower bed and a vegetable patch, which I still enjoy toiling in, and thinking of Elsa. I am sure I would be dead if we didn't leave Germany in '33.

So many enemies of the Nazis were assassinated. Ah, what was the price on my head? What was it in German marks? Don't recall. What was I worth? Ha.

So many intelligent people forsook Germany for America, Great Britain, Canada – any place where one was free to speak his mind. How irrational could a country be: to expel the smart people and replace them with mindless hoodlums? Just because they were Jews, or Gypsies, or Socialists, or homosexuals, or just different from others. At the time, I believe I called it "mass psychosis." It frankly was: how brainless could the Germans be? Oh, those Germans can be monstrously amoral.

We were in California in the winter when Hitler and his henchmen took over. It was our third winter visit to America – I once spoke of these visits as "loafing in paradise." It was warm and dry, while Germany was cold and damp. We made the trip three winters in a row. There would have been a fourth, but: Hitler, January 1933. We returned to Europe but never ever set foot in Germany. We went to Belgium. I was friendly with the Queen, and she gave us a place to stay in the coastal town of *Le Coq sur Mer*, with bodyguards to protect us from the Nazis. I took trips to Great Britain, for lectures on relativity that I had been slated to deliver. They were important lectures that I, oh, oy, how could I forget? I also took a side trip to Zurich to see Tetel – the last time I saw him. I may have felt too that it was going to be the last time. So painful to recall. He took all his pent-up rage out on me. Cataloging all the times I failed him; the forgotten visits; the times I did not take him with me somewhere; my failures to acknowledge his achievements. All I ever did was reprimand him, according to his recollections. He never did anything good enough for me, or so he said. Is all this true? Was I really such a failure as a father? Um, maybe so. I do remember admonishing him for being so sensitive to seemingly every little slight or snub. My telling him to get over it; not to blow everything out of proportion. Yes, I refused to mollycoddle him; that was his mother's function. So, yes, I was not what he wanted for a father. Yet, can I now admit to myself that maybe I was wrong in my lack of rapport with Tetel? That I should have made more of an effort to comply with his needs. Well, at least I *still* keep sending him money for support.

Maybe I should not have made that visit. It made me even more uneasy when I returned to *Le Coq*. Nonetheless, it was peaceful in that sleepy town, but with an undertow of foreboding that still makes me feel creepy as I remember the tension and stress. What if the Nazis had killed me? Would such a killing be deemed an assassination? I was not a politician, but I *was* a public figure. It would have been symbolic for the Nazis to have eliminated me.

Or, what if I had returned to Germany. Would I have been a victim of the mass killings? All this was not an idle threat. I remember my friend Walther Rathenau, who was the foreign minister of Germany, a devoted nationalist like Haber, whose open-seated car was riddled with machine-gun bullets as he drove to work. The right-wing thugs threw in a hand-grenade to make sure this Jew-in-a-high-place was eliminated. June, 1922. Before that, 1921? A right-wing newspaper wrote outright for *my* murder. Later, there followed more threats against me. I spent six weeks in Leiden in 1923 because of death threats in Berlin.

Michele, you were an engineer. You will understand how I remember this minutia because of my love of numbers. At least, I think I am remembering them correctly.

When I returned from Leiden, Elsa and I went on our long Far East tour – not only to lecture and to see the sights afar, but to get away from the frictions and tensions in Germany. We even contemplated moving to America, but did not. Not yet, anyway.

During our return to Europe from the Far East tour, we made a scheduled two-week stop in Palestine. Visited many of the landmarks of the region, such as the remaining ancient Temple wall in Jerusalem. Oh, but what most interested me was the kibbutz movement – those Jewish collective farms based on the communist ideal. At the time, I was flirting with socialism as a reasonable alterative to capitalism. Um, hence my attraction.

At this stage of my life this experience emotionally affected me directly and deeply. Yes, indeed, it was a different Jewish world I met in Palestine, surely a far cry from the life-style of European Jewish culture. I wrote in a letter, as I recall: "The brothers of our race in Palestine charmed me as farmers, as workers, and as citizens." At one point in the tour, among the adulations of a large group of school children and teachers, I called this "the greatest day of my life."

Well, we stopped in Palestine for the inauguration of the Hebrew University, one of my pet charities. I was asked to deliver an address in a temporary building on Mount Scopus in Jerusalem. Oh, I tried to speak in Hebrew – well, it was the right thing to do, since these were probably the first spoken words at the nascent school of learning. I wanted to kick myself for not continuing with the Hebrew instructions leading toward a Bar Mitzvah when I was a pre-teen. Too late. So, from my mouth that day came a botched version of the ancient language, but everyone said they were pleased with what I did – or, in truth, what I tried to do. Oh, well. I continued in French, and so the first lecture at what eventually became the Hebrew University of Jerusalem was delivered by me. I was honored, I remain honored. In my lecture, I outlined the theory of relativity in about ninety minutes. What else?

Sigh.

Relativity, ah, oh, the rain has stopped, and the gardener has resumed his pruning. He leaves footprints in the wet grass that clings to his shoes. What is that blue object he is hanging on a tree? Oh, a birdhouse. He sees me, and is orientating it so that I will get a view of any bird-family that may live in the little blue house, which I can watch coming and going. Ah, that must have been the source of the hammering and such. Humm, he built it himself. How did the paint dry so fast, and in this damp climate? Reminds me: *Le Coq*, there was a birdhouse outside our kitchen window, but I never saw a bird come or go. I was told that the hole was too large for the small size of the birdhouse. A small bird would not have been safe. How do birds know these things? Ah, in *Le Coq* I was safe with my body guards.

Yet: what if the Nazi assassins had breached the Belgium bodyguards and filled me with a barrage of bullets? As if the hole in my Belgium birdhouse had been too large. How would things have changed? Well, not very much for physics, that is. I have not made any major recognized contributions since the mid-1920s, and I still have not brought to fruition my goal of a unified field theory. Unless, of course, I find it before I die. Of course, I think my 1935 paper with Rosen and Podolsky, where we found a fundamental flaw in quantum physics, is important – although only a few physicists agree with us now. Nonetheless, that paper has a glint of immortality, being cited often in the literature and bestowed its own acronym and moniker: the EPR paradox they call it. Um, I probably will not live long enough to see the full impact of that paper.

Then again, there are those papers on gravitational waves that I published in the mid-1930s. I was not the first scientist to put forth the idea of gravity sending off waves throughout space in the same way that electromagnetic waves fill space, an idea pondered in the early years of the century. Ah, but around the time of the final formulation of my general relativity theory, I was the first to give gravitational waves a concrete *mathematical* description. Later, in the mid-30s, I presented a more detailed mathematical formulation, written with Rosen, while we were working on the EPR idea. Nonetheless, I am convinced today that such waves will never be found – not only because they are almost impossible to detect – but mainly because they may not be real. They probably are merely an artifact of mathematical manipulations. Oh, of course, I could be wrong. It would not be the first time I was wrong – I recall my certainty in the 1930s that nuclear mass could only be transformed into pure energy by the stars, not by humans. So, say, in the new millennium, such gravitational waves are found by some extraordinary experimental apparatus that I now cannot even conceive of; what would the headlines say? EINSTEIN IS PROVEN RIGHT AGAIN! – not knowing that, indeed, I doubted their existence, unless some pesky historian spills the beans, as they say. Humm.

Oh, where was I? Ah, yes. Would my murder by the Nazis have been a loss to the world? Ah, probably not, I think. No loss: just a dead Einstein. After all, they were burning my books in the bonfires of Berlin. Um.

burning books
      burning more books
            burning bodies
                  burning more bodies

—Get moving you vermin. Fill that boxcar. Move, move, there's more room, squeeze one more, push. That's it, close the door and lock it. Next car. Get moving you vermin.

Darkness: quiet, slits of light, breathing, eyes adjusting, more breathing, mumbling, children crying.

A loud thud as the train moves forward and a mass of compacted bodies heaves as one mass. Inertia: the law of inertia, so crucial to my theory of relativity. From Galileo: a body at rest tends to stay at rest, resisting this acceleration, so the body – in this case a compacted mass of humanity – experiences a force in the opposite direction. How ironic? Ironic is not an adequate word. How? What?

When I finished my general relativity theory and wrote that long summery article on the subject early in 1916, I immediately wrote a popular book on relativity for an intelligent audience. Looking for an image to explain the relativity of motion, I used the example of a train. Galileo used ships, but I was born in the era of trains. The industrial revolution, steam engines, locomotives, trains. How we experience motion in a train, and ever since, trains are always associated with relativity – perhaps later they will be replaced by airplanes or even rocket ships.

After experiencing a force in the direction opposite to the motion of the train – thus squeezing us further together as the mass pushes against one wall of the boxcar and a small space opens up at the other end – then, as the train reaches a steady speed, the compacted human mass settles into the second part of the law of inertia: a body in motion tends to stay in motion. Once moving, the mass tends to stay in that so-called state of motion. This compacted mass of mumbling, praying, crying, swearing, shivering humanity acts as a whole, unless experiencing a change of speed. Not only will a change in speed in the direction of motion result in a force on this mass, as happened when the train left the station, but any sharp curve left or right will commence a force against a side wall. Just another type of acceleration.

Never did I imagine that my idea of a train in motion to explain relativity would function in my life in such a horrendous way. How could I have?

When I wrote my little book on relativity, which is still in print – but not in Germany, where it was burned in a bonfire – I was trying to explain the theory to any intelligent person. Did any of these Nazis read my book? The word "intelligent" gets caught in my craw, when I contemplate what is happening today – mass madness. How could the Germans believe this nonsense put forth by the fools now running this country? How can people behave en-mass as barbarians in such a brief time? Ugh, it is so easy to be stupid.

In my little book, I use the mental image of trains to compare the experiences of a person in the moving train with another person on an embankment watching the train go by. Comparing measurements of basic parameters: the length of a stick, the weight of a heavy object, the time passing on a clock. The theory predicted differences between the two measurements: the observer on the moving train with the one off the train and on the embankment. So, weight (or mass) and time, for example, are not absolute. What is measured is different for the two observers. Different measurements, different experiences, sense data, information from the senses. Ah, senses. The sense of smell.

Awareness of odors. The smell of livestock slowly gives way to human body odor. Human urine replaces cow piss. Aware of all five senses. Even taste affected. Dry mouth. Minimal saliva has traces of piss and shit, it seems. Oy, it is like a pressure cooker in here. Pressure cooker? What a thought, Margot cooking in the kitchen. How can I find humor in this hell-hole of a boxcar? Yet, luckily for me – did I say luckily? – wrong word. I am up against a wall, not in the middle of the mass, and so I can see through a slit, a crack between the boards. I push my face against the wood and look out at the scenery passing by. The world, moving from right to left: a cityscape gives way to a rural landscape. Occasionally there are farmers working their fields, who stop and look up as the train passes by. What do they see? What can they hear? What do they know? What are they thinking? I am on the train, they on the embankment, different senses, different experiences, different, damned right.

A pastoral scene, viewed from this moving caged hell-hole. Rural tranquility, with a train carrying human-cargo-misery slicing through the greenery. An embodiment of Germanic barbarism on wheels, disquieting the idyll of the Teutonic folk. Folk, Volk, Volkswagen, a cute little car. Nothing cute about people packed tighter than cattle in a boxcar. Am I dreaming? Is this a hallucination? If only it were just a dream. Thrust into a long Wagnerian Operatic nightmare?

*Germanic culture. Dueling and drinking copious quantities of beer. I was busy reading Kant, when my fellow students were engaged in these Teutonic customs. Immanuel Kant, **The Critique of Pure Reason**, first given to me by Max Talmud, then read again when I was studying at Aarau. Drinking Kant, not beer. Ah, Kant, and Beethoven, and Bach, and – and, how could the Germans, proud of their culture, fall so low as to normalize this boxcar to hell? Endlessly quoting Goethe, the way the English quote their Shakespeare.*

More crying, heavy breathing, the stench is getting unbearable. Someone said there is a bucket latrine somewhere in this packet of people. I just wet my pants, and it seems that the incessantly shaking and moaning woman next to me has a bad case of diarrhea. She keeps mumbling something about Gittel: is it she, her mother – or, God forbid, a child? Out of compassion, I would like to hug her, but – oy, it is dripping on my shoe. Elsa complained about these old shoes. Sure, they are worn-

out, but very comfortable. Oh, the stench. When will it end? Don't the German generals at least need these trains for the war? Is it not a waste? – in both senses of this word? I cannot believe I just said that, even thought that. What is thinking, thinking itself, in this bleak space?

Again, pushing my face onto the wall, seeing through the cracks, peering beyond the horizon, looking toward infinity. Beyond all numbers, 1, 2, 3, thousands, millions, more, out to infinity, the largest number. Is it a number? Cantor, the brilliant mathematician, called it a transfinite number. Cantor, his paternal grandfather was Jewish, but his father was a devout Lutheran and so he raised his son, Georg, in the faith. Georg discovered that there was more than just one transfinite number, yes, more than one infinity. Perhaps an infinite number of infinites in this realm of transfinite numbers. What a stretch of the human imagination. Few believed him, and so he was a pariah among mathematicians; but, in the end, his discovery was accepted by the time he died in a mental institution, always convinced he was right because he believed he was approaching an understanding of God – the incomprehensible, the Absolute. Cantor, the pious Lutheran, died before the anti-Semitic madness came to this culmination, with human cargo towed to slavery and death. Otherwise, with a link to Jewish ancestry – and despite all his pious Protestantism – he too would have been swept up in this lunacy. But Cantor died, sadly (luckily?), in a mental institution, yet still believing that beyond the infinite number of finite numbers there was the realm of the infinite number of transfinite numbers, and beyond that there was the realm of the throne of God.

In this sense, his thinking was linked back to the Middle Ages. Moses Maimonides, the most important Jewish philosopher before Spinoza, used the idea of infinity to prove the existence of God, an idea he borrowed from Aristotle. Maimonides, along with his medieval Christian counterpart, Thomas Aquinas, made a rational deduction. Since no logical causal argument can go on forever, there must be an ultimate source of the first cause, and this is God. Peering beyond the horizon toward infinity, am I spying on the throne of God? Ah, yes, God is the infinite ground of Being? Who said that? Where did I hear that? What does it mean: God is the infinite ground of Being? Where do these ideas come from? Any idea, all ideas.

*Seeing ideas in my mind, Kant's **Critique,** the famous first line: "There can be no doubt that all our knowledge begins with experience." I first read it – around age thirteen? – while the other lads were endlessly talking of sports and girls. It is surprising what you can accomplish when you do not waste your time on these things. Although, of course, years later, I caught up on the girls thing.*

*Oh, Kant. The **synthetic a priori** judgment. Knowledge may begin with experience, but it is filtered through the mind, and this involves **a priori** innate categories that produce concepts. Two of which, Kant deduced, were space and time. But I showed in my relativity theory that this is wrong. It is true that knowledge is processed in each of us through internal reasoning and external information, but Kant was wrong about the specifics of how this happens. The ideas of absolute space and absolute time of Kant (which he got from Newton) are instead **relative** entities. This harkens back to the different experiences of those on the train and those on the embankment: different, yes, undeniably so. But I was able to replace the old absolutes with a different set of absolutes, which I called invariants. For example, the speed of light. Unfortunately, my theory became known as the **relativity** theory and although I wanted to change the name to the **invariant** theory – well, by the time I had developed it to that end, it was too late. The damned initial appellation stuck, and there has been confusion ever since. More than confusion. Hostility to my theory resulted from the misconception that I am positing a world with no absolutes; where anything goes, no laws, no morality.*

But relativity is not anarchism. Just because the man in the train does not agree with the man on the embankment about a few things, does not mean that they cannot agree on other things. But this caveat was ignored by the critics.

*Good God, will I later be accused of instigating the fascism of this century because I destroyed the traditional moral order? Where to begin? Not only is my theory not one of relativism, but even if it were, it would not matter, since my theory is about the **physical** world, not the **moral** world. Physics is entirely irrelevant to human behavior – a point that I have stressed again and again. I will continue to defend it. Oh, no need to, I am in this hell-hole of a boxcar, and will surely be going to my death. The physicists will have to straighten this out, without me.*

Oh, we are stopping. The compacted mass of bodies is being forced forward according to the law of inertia, as the train screeches to a stop. A chorus of moaning from the human mass. Shouting outside. Oh Lord, the door opens. The mass expands as everyone alive breathes in a deep volume of fresh air, as almost instinctively the mass separates into individual parts, and the dead bodies are passed along toward the door for, for what? Are the Nazis going to give them a burial, a proper burial, a Jewish burial? Most likely they will be dumped into a hole somewhere.

More live bodies replace the dead bodies, as the door is locked shut, and we proceed further in our journey toward our fate. What? Where?

Still against a wall, I push my face toward a place with a little knothole for me to see out into the passing world. Dark clouds in the distance. A storm approaching? A farmer watches, the man on the embankment, resting on his hoe, having seen the shuffle of human cargo. What does he think? Who will he tell? How will he sleep tonight? Does it even matter? What if? Oh, a jolt backwards, the human mass wants to stay at rest, but the train is saying otherwise – you are going to move forward, whether you like it or not. So, get used to it and go with the motion. Now, the body in motion wants to stay in motion. And it does. The physics of human misery. The inertia of agony. Inertia, from the Latin word for inert – not wanting to move or change. A rock at rest resists a force to move it; it wants to stay in the state of rest. And the bigger the rock, the harder it is to get it moving; for the greater is the force required to get it going, since inertia is proportional to weight. Then, once it gets moving, it wants to stay in this state of motion. Once it is moving, it now requires a force to stop it; the bigger the rock the harder it is to stop it. Think of a moving train. Yes, a very heavy moving object. Can't stop on a dime. Any cow on the tracks will get mowed down; or any person is killed instantly. Humm, trains again; here in a train, the torture train.

Oh, while writing my little book on relativity, and talking about trains moving, I was so innocent, so naïve; but now I am living it in a most horrific way. Looking through the hole, the German countryside, the dense forest in the distance, the world of Teutonic myths, of Siegfried and Brunhilda, inspired Wagner, Hitler's hero, worked with Jews while simultaneously despising Jews, why? Why, oh why? I don't fully approve of Wagner's extension of musical chromaticism, but I understand why he influenced so many modern composers. Extending the range of what was the limited boundary of harmony since Bach and Mozart. Mozart himself broke it a bit, at times, outside the melodic limits. His string Quartet #19 in C-major, the first movement; called, appropriately, "dissonance." Oh, I would love to hear that right now: two-parts, adagio & allegro. Minutes of pleasure in this grief-infested box. Takes me into another realm. Ah, especially the adagio, breaking all the rules, two-minutes of breaking the rules. Opening with the cello playing an ominous series of C's, joined quickly by the viola on A-flat and moving to G, while the second violin comes in on E-flat followed immediately by the first violin on A – thus the early dissonance. It set the stage for others, such as Wagner; but he extended it much further, sort of playing more of the twelve tones of the octave in a given melody, not keeping to the rule of coming back to the dominant, and such. The music sounds dissonant to most of us. I was once told that the American humorist, Mark Twain, explained Wagner's music by saying that it is better than it sounds. Funny, but maybe true, too. Perhaps if I listened more I would appreciate the dissonance. Oppenheimer has been slowly acclimating me to the late Beethoven quartets, which I formerly avoided. Is my ear adjusting to the dissonance? Maybe, yes, maybe.

Good God, here I am remembering jokes in this cage of woe. Why not? A way of coping. I often would lose myself in my work: withdrawing into the solitude of mathematical physics made me oblivious to the external world. I am doing this here, with the help of these little holes and slits in the wall of this heartrending boxcar on this vile train moving through this serene countryside, gawked at by indifferent observers on the embankment. Progeny of the Germanic barbarisms from the Middle Ages, appropriately?

Yes, I plugged away at general relativity as my first marriage was falling apart, and the work was successful – for it came to fruition (relativity, that is, not the marriage), as I derived the fundamental equation of general relativity in November 1915. It also kept my mind away from the depravation of the Great War. So, in this boxcar, sporadically, I can mentally escape this wretchedness, but the stench and moaning bring me back. How can I avoid it? And now the sound of rain. The storm has arrived. Peering through my little hole to the other world, a heavy storm is soaking the fields. Lightning and thunder adding drama to this. Not necessary. I would prefer the Mozart adagio.

Too bad it is pouring rain, I would like to look toward infinity. To lose myself in the mental world of transfinite numbers. To blot out the screaming babies, the crying children, the moaning women, the swearing men. If only it were a clear day, a clear day to see beyond the horizon, to bathe your being in another reality, perhaps to even write a poem. Yes, on a clear day I could write a poem, a poem about, what? Ah, a poem on the, oy! The wheels are screeching, we are thrust forward; the train is decelerating, the mass of humanity forced toward a wall. Is this the end of this agony train? How many dead bodies will they find this time, to dump in a mud hole grave?

Doors open: large dogs snarling, barking, salivating, men with whips, shouting, screaming, yelling at everyone. Who are these creatures? With dogs and whips? Where did the cultivated Germans find these German barbarians to do this dirty work? Yes, the civilized ancient Romans appropriately called the northern Germanic tribes barbarians. Now, here they are, back again, in the 20th century, as if resurrected from graves in the primeval forest of Germania, slavishly submitting to military obedience and savagery, disposing of dead bodies, carting them to a ditch, a mammoth puddle filled with dead bodies, a grave for today's victims of mass hysteria fueled by the rabid racism of demagogues and fools.

Former teenagers, enamored with militarism, marching, dueling – they are now separating the parents and children, everyone a category, none an individual: men, go over there with Siegfried, and women, go there with Brunhilda. Yes, woman soldiers too, wielding whips and barking orders with their large dogs. What else?

I follow Siegfried. We are stripped naked. "Naked came I from my mother's womb and naked will I return." All alike: separating the strong from the weak, who am I? Sticking in the mud –mud, everywhere, more rain, endless rain, cold rain, chilling the already shivering naked body, thunder.

Siegfried shouting, pointing to, who? Me? No, who?
—You, step up here.
—Who, me?

—Step here, come here. What is your name?

—Why do you want me?

—What is your name?

—Me? Name? Goethe, Goethe is my name.

—Vermin, tell me your name.

—No, not vermin. Beethoven. Beethoven is my name.

*—Vermin **is** your name. What else? Tell me.*

—Marrano is my name no, Spinoza, yes, that's it.

—Look vermin.

—Kant, Immanuel Kant.

—Vermin, I want your real name.

—Horst. My name is Horst. It is Horst Wessel. You want to sing a song that I wrote? Let's sing the Nazi song together: ♪♪ "The flag on high. The ranks tightly closed. The ah…"

—You are an uncooperative piece of shit. Wait, I know who you are. You are that Einstein Jew-vermin. I recognize you, your hair, lots of hair. I've seen your picture in newspapers and magazines, something about science or physics or mathematics. Yes, the hair, Einstein, that's it. Al, Alver, Albrecht? Albrecht Einstein? No, that's not it. What is your first name?

—Al, eh, Abe, Abraham. Abraham Einstein.

—So, we have here the famous Jew: Abraham Einstein, right here. We've been looking for you, and now I have you. But you will no longer be Abraham Einstein. You, a scientist, you like numbers. Yes? Numbers? Well, we will tattoo a number on your arm, it will replace your name. No more Abraham. No more Einstein. Only a number. You'll see numbers.

—May I choose the number? I would like a prime number.

—Shut up you fool. Uh, what is a prime number?

—Were you not properly educated in mathematics in the German curriculum? It is a number that is only divisible by itself or the number 1. Such as the number 7. Or uh…

—Shut up vermin. You will see who is the smartest here. Take that, ugh. Go over there to be tattooed by that woman at the table. Go!

—So, Brunhilda is a tattoo artist, I see.

—Shut up and sit down. What are you talking about?

—How does a woman get a job at this camp, with dogs and whips? Do they interview you in the skill of yelling and screaming? What skills do you have, besides tattooing?

—I was a carpenter. Shut up while I put a number on your arm.

—Oh, are you good with a hammer? I want a prime number, as I told your friend Siegfried, over there. And, could you put an $E = mc^2$ on the other arm?

—Shut up you vermin and sit still.

—You Nazis are not very original in inventing insulting names. Vermin, vermin, vermin – that's all I hear. Not too bright, are you? Dummkopfs, dummkopfs, dummkopfs – the lot of you.

—Shut up. Smart shits like you often go directly to the oven.

—Oh, I would like working in a bakery. Kneading dough – good exercise, and a sometimes even sensuous act. Have you ever thought about that? Ah, I'll knead dough, and you'll hammer nails. We'll be a pair.

—Shut up. You make no sense. Are you some sort of clown? Is that what the hair is all about?

—A clown, yes. I lost my funny nose on the train; it fell into a bucket of piss and shit – floating around like a red turd. But I am also a curious clown who asks questions. What I am infinitely curious about is how you barbarians working here can live with this relentless brutality and death – and still sleep peacefully at night? What variety of human beings are

you? Tell me your story. If I cannot begin to understand you, then I cannot understand this whole panoply of cattle cars, whips, dogs, ovens, noise, stench, screaming. Where did they find creatures like you to do this dirty work? If I can understand you, then maybe the seemingly senselessness of it all might offer me an iota of comprehension. Please, I need to know.

—Shut up you fool. Hold still. I need to finish this tattooed number.

—No, I'll fidget. Yes, I'll fidget, so you fuck up my goddamned tattoo. What will happen to you, or me? Can it get any worse?

—I'll use my hammer and nails to hold your arm still, I will!

—Ah, a crucifixion. Brings back memories of my childhood friends. Do you see the irony? What if you refused this job? Does anyone say "No!" to the carnage?

—They go to the oven, immediately.

—Is that it? Is it that banal – mere self-preservation? Enough to turn a mundane mädchen into a sadistic Brunhilda? What does that say about those very few menschen who refuse? Very, very few, it seems. They must be extraordinary.

—Shut up. Done. You almost got nailed, and now you are numbered. No longer, what was your name? Einstein?

—Yes and No. As I stand here, I am neither Einstein nor the number you just tattooed on my arm. Why does this cold rain keep pouring down? All you have here is this old and naked body, with the hair, lots of hair. Now, kneeling in the mud. Heavy rain, does it never stop? You may tattoo this body. You may turn this muddy body into the smoke coming out of that chimney over there. You may bury the ashes, but you cannot destroy Einstein. Damn this freezing rain. This muddy body is not me. I, the real I, the real Einstein cannot be destroyed. I have lived by my thoughts, my ideas, and they will live beyond my puny body. My ideas I transmit over space and time faster than the speed of light. You can neither stop nor

*destroy these ideas. They are beyond your pathetic attempt to destroy me and my people. For that you are nothing, and when you die, your world will die with you. **You** are the vermin, the swine – pathetic, impotent. Take this muddied lump of flesh, on his knees in the mud, mud in my hair, mud in my mouth, freezing in the incessant pouring rain. It is not Einstein, no not Einstein. The real Einstein is…*

—What!!?? What was that loud crash? Dukas! Margot! What was that?

—I am coming Professor. A sudden storm came up. There was a lightning strike, obviously near here. The whole house shook. This storm is frightening, rattling the windows. I wish it would end. Margot and Chico are huddled under a table, shaking at each thunder clap. I am surprised you slept through much of it. You look a bit dazed Professor.

—I need to rest. Just to rest here for a while, just rest. Then we can have afternoon tea. Yes?

—Yes, Professor. You look distressed? Are you okay?

—Yes, and tea, later. Ah, I see the birdhouse has been blown off the tree and it is sitting in a mud puddle, ugh, mud. Oh, before you go, please fetch my little book on relativity. It is there, on the third shelf near the picture of Newton. Thank you. Later, for tea. I need to rest. Rest with my little book on relativity for the intelligent reader. Where are the intelligent readers?

—I will leave you alone with your little book.

Sigh.

Humm. I wrote this popular book in the tradition of Newton and Galileo. They each produced a book trying to explain their new ideas to a general audience. I told Besso I needed to do this too, since the essence of my theory is basically simple.

Ah, Michele, I wrote you about my idea for this little book. You encouraged me, as I recall. But when I finished it I was not very happy with my creation and wrote that I was disappointed in reading the proofs, for my description of the theory was too wooden. Maybe I should leave popular science writing on my theory to others. Did you agree; did you answer me, Michele? Oh, Michele, how we talked about the train imagery to explain relativity. Here I am, pondering that imagery, after this distressing dream of me being caught up in the Nazi extermination machine. If so, I would have died over a decade ago. But here I now sit, and you just left this pitiful world, before me. How long before I depart? Oh, yes, the condolence letter. Well, maybe after afternoon tea. Um.

It has been so long since I picked up my little book on relativity. How disturbing, distressing, even painful, to realize that one of the key visual concepts in my book is an exposition of the experience of someone in a moving train, who compares his perception with someone outside the train. How bizarre: my dream just brought me back to my book, and the train image. How prosaic it is to read here on page 9, where I introduce an observer in "a railway carriage," and compare his observations with another on an embankment. How quaint to read the phrase, here on page 16, "our old friend the railway carriage," and to see it is repeated later on in the book. How was I to know, when I wrote those innocent lines, of the railway carriage as old friend, that it could also be a boxcar full of human cargo? A nightmare, my nightmare, a reality not long ago crisscrossing Europe along railway lines, here, there, and everywhere – trains rolling to a hell on earth.

Elsa and I never returned to Germany after leaving. Hitler never got me. Here I am, still thinking, in the security of America.

But this place, sadly, is feeling less secure. This demagogue, Senator McCarthy, is stirring up irrational fears that remind me of the fascism of Europe before the last war. Something else to worry about, as I go for afternoon tea. Well, instead, the tea comes up here to my study. Ah …

—Professor, Margot and I have prepared tea.

—What is that hammering noise?

—The gardener came out of the rain and is working in the basement.

—Say, why not invite him for tea? Is there enough for the four of us?

—Yes, we can do that. You always had a penchant for schmoozing with the working class. That reminds me of something Dr. Oppenheimer once told me. One day he was looking out his office window and he saw you having a very friendly and animated discussion with one of the maintenance workers at the Institute. He watched for quite some time, trying to decipher or even to guess what you two were so fervently talking about. He meant to ask you the next day, but forgot. He was very unhappy he forgot. He said that you act as if you grew up among the proletariat.

—Well, as one who often felt ostracized, I was cognizant of the shirking of the lower classes by the snooty upper class. Do you know that when I taught in Prague, I was reprimanded by my superior at the University for speaking to the janitors and faculty administrators in the same way? But I never figured out what the problem was. Was I talking down to the administrators, as if they were janitors, or was I speaking up to the janitors, as if they were administrators?

—I suspect the gardener would like that joke. I believe he has a sense of humor. I will see if he can come to tea.

Oh, Michele, I fondly remember Hans, the janitor and handyman, who worked at my father's factory in Munich. I called him, Mr. Hans. He would give me candy, and let me follow him around through all the nooks and crannies of the place. He knew how everything worked, and explained it all to me, although of course he knew nothing of the physics behind it. That I learned later myself. I was more engaged with Mr. Hans than almost any teacher later in school, and perhaps he is a source of my penchant for chatting with the working class. I suspect I had him in mind when I named our first son, Hans. Although we always called our son Hans Albert, seldom just Hans, and other nick-names.

Ah, the rain is slowing to a drizzle. Temperature is up to 49 degrees. A warm front is coming in after the storm. Maybe more pleasant weather ahead. Humm, the birdhouse is gone. I guess the gardener rescued it from the mud. Rescuing from the mud, mud, death camps, Hitler, death threats, exile in Belgium, *Le Coq,* the rooster, the fable of the rooster who saved a sinking ship by crowing till he died, a dead bird, the birds in *Le Coq* …

the birdhouse
        guards watching over me
                birds coming and going

*I see **Le Coq** from the air. Over the North Sea, Bruges in the distance, the cathedral beckoning to come and perch for a rest. Soaring down among the cottages of **Le Coq,** looking for a place to nest. A series of birdhouses set among the trees and near the seashore. Some elaborate, looking like human cottages or apartments or even castles. Different shapes, different colors. Modern, old-fashioned, strange, complex – all reflecting the ingenuity of the makers more than the practicality for us birds. Trying to find a utilitarian birdhouse, the right size and shape to* *make a nest and be safe from predators. To protect myself and my chicks. To be safe near the shore of **Le Coq**. Ah ha, there's one, a simple, pale blue birdhouse, and with the right size hole to keep out trouble, but large enough to raise a family. Perfect: simplicity, order, harmony, as I swoop-down.*

Go inside: Yuck, what a dump! It looked so nice from the outside. Geez, the previous tenants left this place a mess. I took the time to clean up my nest at the house I left last summer, but these birds were real slobs. Must be one of those other species. You cannot trust them for anything. They are not like us, that's for sure. Should I take the time to get this joint shipshape, or should I try another house? Humm, let's see ...

Oh, I must have dozed off yet again. What!? Dreaming of being a bird! – good grief. How trite. Oh, well, can't Einstein have a banal dream? Does everything have to be profound? I guess not. It's a dream, not a work of literature. Yet, what does it mean? Protecting my young? From *Le Coq* I visited Tetel. Is this about my failure to protect him? Humm, can I not let this go? Probably not, it seems.

And, what kind of bird was I? How does one know? A species is usually only attracted to the same species, or even a sub-species. I guess my dream was not long enough to find out what type of bird I was. It would have been intriguing to know, and let's say I was attracted to a female spotted from afar, and maybe even, ah, I hear the afternoon tea party coming to my study.

—Professor, here is your tea. Margot and I have brought the gardener, as you requested. Meet Mr. Buchanan.

—Doctor Einstein, it's an honor to meet you, Sir.

—Nice to meet you too. Call me Abe.

—Professor, what are you talking about? What is this Abe name?

—Miss Dukas, did I not tell you that when I was born I was supposed to be Abraham Einstein, but my parents opted for Albert, since Abe was too Jewish sounding for their assimilated German mentality?

—I do not believe you ever told me that, Professor.

—Mr. Buchanan, I was dreaming, er, thinking about birdhouses, and I recalled a birdhouse outside the house where we stayed in Belgium in 1933. I was told that there were no birds inhabiting the house because the hole was too large for the size of the house, and the birds knew they would not be safe nesting there. How do they know? How do you know what size hole to make?

—Doctor Einstein, I use three different mental patterns for small, medium, and large birdhouse, with three different sized holes. All have been friendly to birds. As far as I know, no bird rejected my birdhouses. And my houses are used every season.

—There must be a formula for this. A given ratio between, say, the volume of the house verses the diameter of the hole. It is a problem involving optimums. Uses simple calculus.

—Well, simple for you, Sir. I just use my mental pattern that I learned as a boy, but I guess it could be done by some math formula.

—You are a gardener, birdhouse maker, what else do you do, Mr. Buchanan?

—Sir, I am what some call a jack-of-all-trades. My dad was very handy with his hands, and taught me lots of what I know. He had a little workshop in our home. Many of the tools he made himself.

—What was his day job?

—He was a porter on the train, the usual job for men of his generation. But I could not see myself in such as job, forced to be so nice – "yes, Sir, no Sir" – to those who obviously looked down on me. I wanted some control over what I was doing. So, after the war I tried my hand in the gardening and general repairs business, thanks to my dad's teachings.

—What did you do in the war?

—Well, I usually don't talk about this, but if you're interested.

—I am curious, and have the time to listen, since I am making no more progress on my unified field theory. Um, uh, that was a joke. Please go on.

—Sir, I was in the 761st tank battalion, which became known as the Black Panthers – um, for obvious reasons. We were key soldiers in the Battle of the Bulge. We spent six months pushing back the Germans. It was an awful experience, and I still get nightmares, but we helped defeat the Nazis. For that I get some satisfaction.

—Did you come home as a war hero?

—Ah, Sir, that's another story. You see, we were living in Columbus, Tennessee, and …

—Columbus, Tennessee! During the race riots, as they were called?

—Yes, Dr. Einstein, the very place.

—You know, I signed onto the National Committee for Justice in Columbus, Tennessee, headed by Eleanor Roosevelt. I was appalled by what I heard. But please, tell me what you know. You were there!

—I was, Sir, I was. Instead of coming home to cheering crowds, we came home to the rebirth of the Ku Klux Klan and lynchings. In February of 1946 a veteran and a white shopkeeper got into an argument and it led to a hostile reaction from the white community and a reaction from the black community. State troopers were called in and they took sides. They attacked the black district with submachine guns and destroyed every black business in a four-block square area, near where we lived. They arrested over a hundred men. The lawyer defending our men was almost lynched.

—Was your family safe?

—We could hear the shooting, but we stayed inside our home and were not directly affected by the events, although my mum was traumatized by all of it. Today she still jumps at almost any loud noise. It was a critical event in my life, and changed forever my feelings about this country, especially towards most white folk. Since I live here, I'm forced to deal with them, but I assess them one-at-a-time. There are many good people – like you – and my hope is that more will someday soon learn to deal with this problem. My family reads the black papers and I know that you have supported our cause. I remember hearing my dad tell me that you gave your support to the Scottsboro Boys in Alabama in, was it '31, or so? I was around ten-years-old.

—Oh, yes. It was a case of about nine Negro lads falsely accused of raping a white girl, and they were facing the death sentence. I was still in Germany, but it gave me a forewarning of what to expect if I moved to America. So, the discrimination was no major surprise when I moved here.

—Sir, is it true that the great opera singer, Marian Anderson, stayed in your home when she was in town giving a concert, because she couldn't rent a room at any hotel in Princeton?

—Yes, in the late-1930s, she stayed with us. We have remained life-long friends. Indeed, she was here again in January, this year.

—Oh? I wish I knew. I believe that you are also a close friend of another great singer, Paul Robson, who I just love to hear sing, well, to sing anything. Did you know that he was born here in Princeton?

—Yes, our friendship too began when he was here at a concert, some-time in the mid-1930s. He told me about growing up in this town, with the endemic racism. We presently are co-chairs of the American Crusade to End Lynching. It is hard to believe that this heinous crime has not abated, and that murderers continue their crimes, often with impunity in the South.

—According to the black papers, Robson is being viciously attacked by Hoover's FBI as a communist. And you, too?

—Yes, Robson told me he believes that Hoover's men are constantly watching him. His concerts are cancelled. They took away his passport in 1950 so he cannot give concerts overseas, where they love him. It is a disgrace.

—Someday, I hope, this country will look back and be ashamed at what is happening now.

—So true. I left Nazi Germany because of things like this being everyday life. People spying on their neighbors. There, the enemy was Jews, here it is communists. Them and us. In 1948 I spoke out for clemency for the Rosenbergs, but it was futile. This Senator McCarthy is fanning the flames. He is a fascist, but few see this. But I tell things like they are. I am not afraid to speak out. Blind nationalism: it is an infantile disease. I lived through it in Germany, during and after the First War, and it turned me into a pacifist in the 1920s. Well, that is, until the rise of Hitler, when I had to rethink and modify my steadfast pacifist view. Anyway, this has been a long-winded digression from, where were we?

—I believe, Sir, the topic of my dad came up – that he taught me to be the handyman I am today.

— You mentioned that your mother is still alive, is your father?

—No, he died ten years ago of heart failure. But he lives within me, as I enjoy fixing and making things. Real things. So, I can see the results.

—I also make and fix things, but they are not tangible in the way you use the term. My theory of relativity was in many ways a fixing up of Newton's old theory, since it was incomplete regarding things going very, very fast. And for my theory of cosmology, I have been called the maker of a universe. George Bernard Shaw said that at a banquet for me many years ago. So, I guess I make and fix models or theories, which are the things of physics. But I do appreciate your point of view. When I was a child I was enamored with my father's electrical shop, with its generators, dynamos, and other very material objects. I have great respect for those who can build and work such things. It helped me when I got my first real steady job, working in a patent office, where I needed to assess whether potential inventions were viable. For some time, I thought of being an engineer; indeed, my father wanted me to follow that career, but I became obsessed with physics, and eventually theoretical physics. I do recall, however, that I made a little cable car for my son, Hans Albert, as a child. I used matchbooks and string, and he loved it. He has told me he remembers it as a favourite toy. But I guess that was the extent of my engineering career, except for some inventions that I patented myself or with others. For example, with a fellow physicist, we invented a refrigerator with no moving parts. It was to be much quieter than those with the noisy pumps. But it never was a commercial success. So, except for these occasional flights into the practical realm, mostly my mind is and was in the clouds, as many people would say.

—Is that a reference to Aristophanes, Dr. Einstein?

—Well, ah, yes, it is, I presume. What a surprise. You must be a keen reader Mr. Buchannan.

—I enjoy the old Greek plays. They show much insight into human nature, which is still relevant today. I think that is why Freud borrowed from Greek mythology for ways to explain his ideas. Do you agree?

—Would you believe that I was thinking the same thought earlier today, when I was contemplating, uh, I can't recall the context, um.

—I am also a sort of history buff. But I find much historical writing stiff. Book reviewers often complain of such writing being too academic, or dry, or both. I agree: that is why I am attracted to works of historical fiction. Such books are better at keeping my attention, while still giving some knowledge of the past that I want. Sir, have you read any historical novels?

—I do not recall reading any book in the genre, but it does get me thinking about my own biography. I know that my legacy will live on in writings about me. So far there have been a few attempts at full biographies. The first that comes to mind is that by my friend Philipp Frank, who took over my job in Prague after I left. He wrote a *Life and Times* book in the late 1940s. Also, my student and eventual colleague Leopold Infeld wrote a biography around 1950, with the emphasis on my influence in physics. Miss Dukas and I got him out of Poland during the Nazi era, with a position here at the Institute. When the money ran out he and I wrote a book together, the popular little *The Evolution of Physics* that sold enough to keep him going for years, until he got a position at the University of Toronto in Canada around 1939. His research was not on nuclear physics but for some reason it was thought that he was an expert, and also a communist sympathizer. In fact, he was a peace activist like me, and a staunch anti-communist as well. But Canada after the last war, like America, was irrational about supposed communist bogeymen everywhere, and Infeld was classified as a traitor. He went back to Poland in 1950, becoming a professor at the University of Warsaw. He just signed the Russell-Einstein Manifesto. Do you know about it? Anyway, who else wrote a biography of Yours Truly? Of course, there is the mid-1940s book by Marianoff, Margot's short-timed husband. He called it, *Einstein: An Intimate Study of a Great Man.* Margot and Dimitri came to Princeton in the mid-1930s, but they later divorced. I believe he married her just to get access to me. I have been rereading it recently. I don't know why, but it caught my eye on the shelf and I could not put it down for some reason. Anyway, there is also the book by my other son-in-law, Rudolf Kayser, who married Margot's older sister, Ilsa; his book was published much earlier, around 1930, under the more English sounding pseudonym, Anton Reiser, since he wrote it in English and wanted to appeal to that audience. He was a Jewish journalist, editor, author, and an important literary critic during the heyday of the Weimar republic in the 1920s. He lost his job in 1933, and after Ilsa died the next year, he moved to America. He is now teaching at Brandeis University. Over the years Kayser and I had much in common to talk about, such as Spinoza. We keep in touch. I wrote the *Introduction* to his splendid book on Spinoza. Where is that book? See, uh, over there Mr. Buchanan.

—Yes, I see it, Sir. Um, is your library in any real order or are the books rather irregularly placed?

—Yes. By that I mean that they are random to you but I know where everything is – or, at least, where most of them are. Miss Dukas will have a gargantuan task cataloging my library after I am gone.

—I see, Sir, that Kayser's book on Spinoza is right besides Spinoza's *Ethics*. I heard it is a difficult read. Maybe Kayser's book would be a better place to begin.

—Ah, Spinoza's *Ethics* is his masterpiece. What an extraordinary reading experience: logical propositions, strung together, guiding the reader through a mental journey on God, the mind, human emotions, and freedom. For a man of my temperament, it was a riveting experience. The same format as Euclid's geometry but with an entirely different content.

— Maybe I should just dive into it, and see how the journey goes.

—Yes, Mr. Buchanan, why not. I recall that Kayser's book is more on Spinoza's life and times. Let's see. What did I say in the *Introduction*? Humm, only two-and-a-half pages, humm, listen to my language: the frightful events of our times, despondency, disillusionment, spiritual conflict, the loss of confidence in the progress of man, misery, distress, a search for inner peace and security, spiritual distress, skepticism. Humm, two-thirds into the *Introduction*, and finally Spinoza is mentioned. I see him as grappling with a similar spiritual distress or conflict as many men today. His deduction of the causal certainty underlying all of nature was a "remedy for fear, hate, and bitterness" – and so he is a model for us today. Well, well, humm. I see that I was still rather traumatized by the events of the last war. The year was 1946, the war had just ended and I was writing about the psycho-social state of mind following the slaughter on the battlefields in Europe and on the islands of the Pacific, culminating in the destruction of Hiroshima and Nagasaki by nuclear bombs. Looming large in my mind, no doubt, was surely the genocide against my fellow Jews. You know, I lost at least two relatives that I know of in the mass murder: a cousin Lina in Auschwitz, and another cousin Bertha at Theresienstadt. So, how did we get onto this topic? Oh, where was I? What were we talking about, Mr. Buchanan?

—Well, um, historical fiction, I guess, Sir.

—Oh, yes. Maybe somewhere in the future someone will take the chance and pen a biography of me in the historical fiction genre. A novel about me. Well, I have been a very novel person.

—Ha, that's certainly true, Sir. But I foresee a problem.

—You do, Mr. Buchanan? Please tell.

—Well, you are a famous scientist working in a most murky branch of physics, as far as I know. Not only are the concepts often cloudy but there is much tricky math – and so many people have a fear about math, almost a phobia. My guess is that many keen readers of novels fit into this category. I'm sure that putting equations in a novel would scare off many, maybe most, possible readers. I'd guess that an equation in any book probably does the same.

—Humm, I suspect you are right. Indeed, I am aware of this. I used math in my little book on relativity that I wrote for a general audience right after I finished the theory in 1916. I believe, as a result, it was generally read only by those with a scientific background. By which I mean that they were not only the ones who bought the book, but who actually read it through. So, when Infeld and I wrote the popular *Evolution of Physics* in the 1930s, we purposely avoided any mathematics. There are diagrams, lots of them, but no equations. Not even $\mathbf{E = mc^2}$, believe it or not. And it sold well. It is still selling today. Yes, I believe you are right.

—Also, is not the actual doing of science mainly boring, at least to the non-scientific person? Lots of dull calculations and such, with a few, if any, so-called eureka moments?

—Yes and no. Let me explain. The key question is: how do you properly write a novel about scientific research? The important things that happen take place in the slow, methodical work that one does daily. All of which, for me as a theoretical physicist, is taking place in my brain. Oh, I know, people like to believe that it is all dramatic, with flashes of inspiration, as if from heaven. Yes, there are such moments, of sorts, but it is seldom the way it is portrayed as a so-called eureka event in books and plays and movies. Often it involves an interesting idea that comes to mind during a rigorous chain of calculations or such, and which is briefly considered but dropped for the moment – only to come back, later, when you realize that it may indeed be important. I believe that science historians have shown that there are truly very few eureka events in history – at least in the way they are portrayed in popular re-creations. The real history of my scientific life would be boring to the general reader, so I suspect only a naïve writer would take a stab at an historical novel about me and my science.

—Yes, it may take a gutsy guy, or maybe a very innocent person to take a crack at a historical novel about your life. Who knows?

—I wonder what parts of my life the plucky author will fictionalize. Humm, let me guess, perhaps …

—Dr. Einstein, I'm sorry, but I need to get back outside to prune more bushes and trees now that the rain has stopped and it's getting warmer. I very much enjoyed this little chat, Sir. And thank you Miss Dukas for the tea.

—It was both pleasant and enlightening talking with you Mr. Buchanan. Come by again, soon, I want to explore further what you mean by a mental pattern for your birdhouses. The idea intrigues me.

—Sir, I look forward to the next chat, because I want to ask you about your honorary degree from Lincoln University.

—Ah, yes, a marvelous visit. I was so pleased that I accepted it. Yes, we'll talk about it over tea and those little things that Margot makes. Oh, wait, Mr. Buchanan, do you like ice cream?

—Why, yes, of course.

—Well, I once met the owner of the Breyers Ice Cream Company while taking the ferry from New Jersey to Manhattan, and we struck up a friendly conversation. Not surprisingly we talked about ice cream and I revealed that consuming large quantities of his product was a particular vice of mine. Well, since then I have been receiving 25 liters of it every month. We have quite a supply of many varieties – a virtual store. And, with these poor freezers on today's refrigerators, it is difficult keeping the ice cream from melting. Now, if only the refrigerator I invented had come to fruition, oh, well. Miss Dukas, let Mr. Buchanan pick out whatever he wants.

—Yes, Professor. I will give you your choice, Mr. Buchanan. I will see you before you leave today.

—Thank you, Miss Dukas, and thank you, Dr. Einstein.

—Yes, enjoy the ice cream, and Miss Dukas, don't forget tonight for dessert.

—Of course, Professor. Ice cream for dessert.

Sigh.

A Solitary Smile

Where was I? What does that mean? "Where was I?" What a silly question. I am right here, still in my comfy chair. After afternoon tea, with oh, yes, ice cream for dessert. Humm, ice cream

ice cream

        cream

             creamy

                  dreamy

                        dream

Dreaming, dreams within dreams. I remember once dreaming that I woke up from the dream, and discovered that I was still dreaming. I tried to wake myself up again; and when I did, Margot was there, so I had her pinch me to prove that I was fully awake, and I pinched her back, and we had a big laugh. We laughed so hard. But it was not the biggest laugh with Margot. Another time I told her that when I was a student at the Poly, a physics teacher suggested that I change to another subject, such as law or medicine, that I was not cut out for physics. I replied that I still wanted to make the effort in physics, since I was not interested in those other subjects. When I told that story to Margot she kept repeating "not cut out for physics," over and over, and she laughed harder than I think I ever heard her laugh – so hard that she fell off her chair, and kept laughing on the floor, with Chico licking her face. She, like Chico, is always more comfortable on the floor, preferably under a table.

Oh, but then there was that time I was taking a bath, and I was in the bathroom so long that Margot came and knocked on the door to see if I were well. Sitting in the warm bath I did not fall asleep, but instead I began contemplating a physics problem, and got so engrossed that I forgot where I was. When she knocked, she asked if anything was wrong. I briskly replied that everything was fine, and queried as to why was she bothering me at my desk. Well, that led to a strange exchange, until I realized that I was not at my desk but in the bathtub. Not surprisingly,

103

*Margot broke into deep laughter, so much so that she continued to laugh spontaneously at times for the next few days. She still recalls that incident whenever I mention taking a bath. But I frankly **did** believe I was at my desk at the time.*

So, now, if I go downstairs to the music room and play the piano, will that prove I am no longer dreaming? Humm.

3. Late-afternoon

"The fear of communism has led to practices that have become incomprehensible to the rest of civilized mankind and expose our country to ridicule. How long shall we tolerate politicians, hungry for power, who are trying to gain political advantage in such a way?"
—Einstein, February, 1954, written to a society of Jewish lawyers upon receiving a merit award

—Wake up, father. What were you dreaming? Your fingers were moving as if you were playing the piano. Were you?

—Yes, playing the piano, in my sleep. Mozart, or was it Bach? How long was I sleeping? Am I awake? Pinch me.

—Oh, not that again. Yes, you are awake.

—Maybe I will go down to the piano. I have always – well, at least, sometimes – had major breakthroughs in my work on physics while improvising on the piano. I could use a breakthrough.

—Well, no breakthrough right now father, for Dr. Nathan just came in to see you. You know, he looks so distinguished with those round-rimmed glasses, his slightly balding forehead, and the ever-present serious look on his face. Why, pray tell, is he still single? He is a bit short, but not much shorter than you. Oh, he is coming up the stairs.

—Um, that's nice. Ah, Otto, so nice to see you. How goes? Say, don't you ever wear anything but a three-pieced suit? Do you sleep in one?

—I guess my apparel is always quite a contrast to your, how should I say, uh, slovenly wardrobe? Anyway, I am sorry I missed your birthday last Monday; I guess I am a week late. You will find a package on the piano bench downstairs in the music room.

—The birthday? Oh, it was anarchism on the front lawn with endless reporters whom I avoided. Sit down, it is never too late. Who wants to celebrate birthdays anymore?

—I understand. What is this you are writing? I see a blank sheet on your desk that looks as if it is seeking some scribbles.

—My old friend Besso recently died, and all day I have been trying to write a letter to his sister and son. But I cannot even get started. I keep reminiscing about my life, remembering things. Did I ever tell you about our illegitimate daughter, Lieserl? Few know about this.

—Yes, and we should keep it that way. No need to dredge up unsavory details of your life.

—But, Otto, it *is* me. I know I am not the saint that the popular press makes me out to be. Just because I have a halo of hair. I am afraid that after I die, you and Miss Dukas will try to protect my image: sort of two "keepers of the flame," as they say. Anyway, my day has consisted of daydreaming, falling asleep, strange dreams, and having imaginary conversations with Besso, what a day!

—Sounds delightful to me. The stuff of novels. The life of the famous Einstein – in one day. An instant best seller!

—Funny you should say that. This afternoon I had a conversation with the gardener about this very thing – a historical novel about my life.

—Well, I hope that I am in it. Did I play a significant role in your life since you moved to America?

—Otto, you were, oh, here is Dukas with the tea and cookies or whatever.

—Dr. Nathan, you were very important to all of us. When we landed in America and were living in the Peacock Inn here in Princeton; you came to our assistance. Without you we would have been lost.

—Miss Dukas is correct, Otto. We don't know how we could have settled in so smoothly without your support. We have become such close friends, so much so that I made you the sole executor of my will.

—Yes, about five years ago, and I am honored, Albert.

—Also, don't you or Dukas forget my request that after I die, I want to be cremated, and my ashes are to be scattered in an unknown place. Otherwise I could turn into one of those medieval saints, where their body parts become relics. Those reliquaries in Catholic churches have fingers, hearts, and God knows what organs stuffed into the ornate vessels. If they could, my devotees would probably save my brain. Um, but they could just as well save my penis, which I used about as much in my younger and productive days. Please, cremate me; all of me. I do not want there to be a gravesite acting as a place of pilgrimage. I do not want to be a relic, even if I am considered in some quarters as a kind of secular saint. Oh, and the same applies to this house on Mercer Street. Margot will get it, and she is not to turn it into a museum. It must remain a private residence, indefinitely.

—Yes, Albert, Helen and I will do as you request. You know this. Indeed, I am so glad I met you here in America. Strange that we did not know each other previously in Berlin. Oh, well, that was silly to say – every Jew did not know every other Jew. Although, everyone knew who you were, Herr Doctor Professor Einstein.

—Well, in fact, Otto, I had heard of you: the well-known economist working in Berlin, a trusted advisor to the government. In time, I suspect, we would have met, since we both were attracted to socialism and pacifism. You, even more so than I. But then Hitler and, well, we both fled to America. Thank goodness you got that initial job at Princeton University.

—Yes, it helped me to settle in more quickly. And eventually to meet you. But the job did not last.

—I am sure you were fired because of the covert anti-Semitism here. This town is saturated with white upper-class gentile snobbery, bigotry, and downright racism. Otto, you should have a chat with my gardener.

—Well, in the end, I have been able to get appointments at other universities in this country, and I especially enjoyed my time teaching at Howard University, speaking of your gardener.

—And, speaking of pacifism. I have been corresponding with Bertrand Russell. He wrote me in February about putting forth a manifesto warning the world of nuclear annihilation. He wanted about six well-known scientists to sign it. I wrote back quickly agreeing with him completely. But I suggested that about a dozen signatures would be better. I obviously recalled – was it only three? – the few who signed the 1914 anti-war Manifesto that I helped to write in Germany at the start of the hideous war. So, I suggested to Russell that we should write to Bohr and my friend Infeld, now at the University of Warsaw. Russell and I have been corresponding back and forth since. We are revising the document and such.

—A splendid idea, Albert. A Russell-Einstein Manifesto, or is it an Einstein-Russell Manifesto? No matter. I look forward to seeing what comes of this. Which reminds me: did I ever tell you that I believe your legacy in the long run – that is, long after we are both gone – will be more about your social and political theory than your physics? I've been thinking about this recently. I know that many historians have dismissed your pronouncements on political and social topics as naïve, saying that you are out of your league; that you should stay with your science and leave the other analyses to experts in these other fields. I, however, disagree. I find your scrutiny of society and politics deep and probing. Your physics may be replaced or corrected by later theories, but what you say about the social order will prove to be true, and will endure. Unless, of course, we have nuclear annihilation.

—I am afraid of this. The present rush to build bigger bombs is collective madness. Someday, with very large nuclear arsenals, one country is going to launch a missile, if political tensions get to a breaking-point.

—True, uh, military generals are trigger-happy. And there will be counter attacks, and, I know this all sounds trite, but I believe it is a real possibility. Political decisions seem to be motivated more by emotions than by reason.

—Yes, just look at the present situation in this country. We have to deal with this fascist McCarthy and the obsession with communism from him and the House Committee on Un-American Activities, which everyone calls HUAC. And Hoover and his FBI, they are just as dreadful. Together there is a Hoover-HUAC alliance. Since moving here, I have detected a deep strain of anti-intellectualism in American culture. The present craziness is a manifestation of it, I believe. You know, I would not be surprised if my house was being wiretapped and my phone monitored right now. Maybe you, too? Eh, Otto?

—Speaking of which, the State Department still has not granted my request for a passport, which has been dragging on since December 1952. But last week a judge directed the government to give me a hearing. We'll see what comes of that. All this probably has something to do with my association with socialism when still in Europe. The fools in this country do not know the difference between socialism and communism. They maintain that if I leave this country I might assassinate the President of France. Where do they come up with this babble? I am fighting it in court. I just hope they do not drag me before their damn HUAC. I would assert that no Congressional committee has the right to inquire into the political beliefs of American citizens. God knows, I did not flee German fascism to end up in jail in America. What a century we are living in! You know, I was recently glancing at your popular book that you gave me in the late-30s on *The Evolution of Physics*, and in the dedication, you wrote: "To my dear friend Nathan, in an evil time." How appropriate.

—I will support you, Otto. You know that. Just as I have written in support of so many others who are hounded by right-wing radicals. This fanatical fear of communism has led to behavior in this country that is sometimes incomprehensible to other civilized nations. It is strange and frightening how we tolerate power hungry politicians, who often take advantage in this way. In fact, I was thinking yesterday that even fame is no shield from this. Look at Charlie Chaplin. I met him on our annual visits to Caltech in the early 1930s, before Hitler. Elsa and I were the honored guests at the premier of his movie, *City Lights*. When we entered the theater, a large crowd was cheering us, and I said to him, "What does it all mean?" His reply was: "They are cheering me because they under-stand me; they are cheering you because they do not understand you." I think this was one of the most profound insights into my theory that I have heard in my lifetime. It rings true, doesn't it? Yes, mass-man is very strange. Anyway, I thought of Chaplin because when his latest movie, *Limelight,* came out a few years ago it was banned in California, and many theaters across the country refused to show it. It was because he was branded a communist. He was almost called before HUAC, and being so harassed, he moved back to England, the place of his birth. When he left, a motion was passed by the American government refusing him a return entry. The movie was premiered in London. He remains there. Or think of Oppenheimer: he is surely famous, and look at the deep troubles the American fascists are giving him.

—Speaking of Oppenheimer, I believe I hear his voice downstairs talking with Miss Dukas. Are you expecting him?

—No, but he does stop in now and then.

—Well, I have finished my tea and cookie-things, so I will make room for Oppie. I just wanted to drop off the birthday package, uh, it's on the piano bench.

—Thank you. I am so glad you stopped by. Come again soon, and let me know if I can write something in support of you.

—Thank you too. Yes, I know you are always there for me. I hope you make some progress in that letter to the Besso family. Good-by Albert. Till the next time.

—Yes, Otto, in this world or the next.

—Well, hello, Dr. Oppenheimer, it has been awhile. I suppose you left your Stetson hat at the door?

—Oh, Otto Nathan. It is pleasant to see you. No, I left my hat on the piano bench beside a package.

—The package is my belated birthday gift, but putting the hat beside it is not a good idea, I think. Chico may be able to grab it and use it as a bone. I'll place it on a higher level on my way out.

—Oh yes, Otto, you are right. Those wire-haired terriers can be a terror this way. Incidentally, speaking of terror, I hear that you too are having problems with the government. Maybe we should commiserate together sometime.

—Yes, I suppose we would have much to talk about, or rather to complain about. Call me if you get to New York.

—I will, surely, yes, I will.

—Oh, J.R., you are here again, and with another record, I see. Do you want some tea and Margot's little things?

—Yes, and Yes. Another record, and some tea and dainties.

—More Mahler?

—No. Poor Nathan, accused of communist activities. But he is such a benign man; always serious. Doesn't smoke, doesn't drink, almost an ascetic. No trouble to anyone. Although, like you, he is drawn toward political socialism. By the way, I recently read that Mahler was a closet socialist. But Albert, you are out-of-the-closet, openly articulating the ideology.

—True. I always abhorred the idea of a class structure in society. That's why I was attracted to socialism, and communism, at least in principle. In practice, however, communism, well that's another thing – just a different form of dictatorship. Also, I was never enamored with the idealizing of the lower classes. You know, that obligatory righteousness of the proletariat that pervades much of Marxist theory. I am deeply suspicion of mass-man, with its herd mentality. I saw it in action in Germany, and it scared the shit out of me. Most working-class people are prone to simplistic explanations and easy prey for opportunistic politicians. I see it happening here today. My socialism is more of an economic socialism, not a political one. I believe in universal economic equality. All citizens deserve access to the commonweal of the land. Large gaps between the rich and poor are unethical, at least; perhaps even immoral. But that's where my socialism ends. In other ways, I am an elitist. All of us are not equal intellectually, for example – even where we have universal education. How could I not be an intellectual elitist?

But, of course, you know all this. You also innocently flirted with communism as a student and it has come back to haunt you in this paranoid climate of America today. Hoover and McCarthy in some ways remind me of Hitler and Goebbels. It is as if the German calamity is repeating itself here in America: people acquiesce without resistance and align themselves with the forces for evil, opening themselves up to a form of stupid tyranny. When I speak out on this, I am seen as a sort of *enfant terrible.*

—But surely, Albert, you are overstating this. Indeed, exaggerating. Look what recently occurred: the radio journalist, Edward R. Murrow, broadcast a critical report about McCarthy, which eventually led to the Senate censuring the senator in March of last year.

—True, but the anti-communist mass hysteria has not diminished. The witch-hunting continues and the lives of loyal citizens are being ruined. Good Lord, J.R., you would think that having been humiliated by McCarthy's witch-hunt, forced to testify and confess about your student political ventures before the House Committee, censured by the Senate, and then lost your security clearance last year – after all this over the last six or so years, I do not understand why you do not see how evil your beloved country can be.

—It probably has something to do with my American roots in the Enlightenment and the belief in the perfectibility of man. This, plus the continuing role of Pragmatism in various guises. The result is a mode of nationalistic identity that you do not seem to grasp.

—No, or yes, I do *not* understand it. My experience in Europe, especially Germany, was an exposure to a form of blind nationalism that I lived through during and after the First War. It was not based on the perfectibility of man, as I see it. Rather, I saw the rude masses driven by dark passions that dominated them, and even the governments that represented them. It was not a pretty picture, nor did it foster a very optimistic view of human behavior. From my viewpoint, I see you as being a victim similar to my friend Fritz Haber. He was the great hero of the First War, and also a deep German nationalist in the 19th century tradition. But the Nazis vilified him, turning the war hero into an enemy and a non-person. Sound familiar? You were the leader of the project that built the bombs that ended the war with Japan. A war hero too. But look what the anti-communist fools in this government have done to you.

—Well, yes. There are parallels; I cannot refute that. But …

—But what? There are always "buts" when I raise serious doubts about the precarious state of American democracy. Have you thought deeply about how the Negroes are treated in large sections of this country? They live in a pre-Civil War culture, minus the slavery – and they are still being lynched.

—I must say, Albert, that it was a noble gesture when you accepted an honorary degree from Lincoln University in the 1940s, our oldest black college. And your penetrating essays over the years on the social status of the Negro in this country have shamed us all. Your judgment that segregation is a "disease of the white people" is a biting testimonial against the injustice still permeating this country.

—Noble, shmoble. The white press barely mentions it, whereas it is front page news in the Negro papers everywhere. How much longer can this problem continue to fester?

—Ever since your experience in Germany – from your youth, I believe – you have been an anti-nationalist. You have a profound sense of internationalism that I applaud. I wish I could embrace it more than I do. But I did not grow up in Germany and, well, this is just another way that we are different. I have an unwavering American identity. You may call it blind nationalism, but I see it with eyes wide open, I hope.

—I think this nationalism may be filling a psychological void in you that was a result of your youthful rejection of Judaism. You certainly have not made the adult leap that I made with a robust cultural Jewish identity. I have openly championed myself as a Jew, whereas you try to hide it, it seems.

—True, I guess. By the time I was at Harvard, I was an unconditionally secular American, and maybe my attraction to the Hindu Classics was part of a search for some iota of spirituality. I studied Sanskrit and read the *Bhagavad-Gita* in the original language. I considered it a major world classic of literature. Still do.

—Humm. We, both Jews, but different backgrounds. What do you think, for example, was a source of your sense of ethical behavior? Were you schooled in Judaism as a youngster?

—I never seriously thought about this, but I suspect that an answer may be found in my time spent as a student in something called the Ethical Culture Society that my parents were active in, and so I attended their special School. Probably that had a more profound influence on me than I might otherwise admit. Are you familiar with it?

—Why yes, of course. I knew one of the founders of the Swiss Ethical Culture Society. Gustav Maier, a friend of the family from my birth place, the town of Ulm: a banker and a pacifist, and a socialist too. He later moved to Zurich and even helped me get into the Swiss Polytechnic, since I was applying at an early age. He also set up my lodging with the Wintelers in Zurich. In fact, Jost Winteler, the father, was a co-founder of the Society with Maier. During my years at the Poly I often visited with Maier and attended some meetings of the Society. I agreed, and still do, with many of their principles. His book on the history of economics and society in Europe had a strong influence on my thoughts on such matters, and I still hold to his interpretation today, especially his view that this history should culminate in a socialistic society. Only with such a grand finale could real justice prevail in the world.

—Well, I attended the School from Grade Two through High School, and was fully inculcated in their liberal beliefs. A belief in progress, a strong moral code, the role of duty (you know, the *noblesse oblige*), a concern with the social welfare of all citizens – all within a framework of high academic standards. The compassionate teachers helped me, in part, to overcome my shyness. I suppose it is no surprise that I became a scientist-statesman in the postwar years.

—Who knew that we had this in common, J.R.? You know, I wrote a note of support to the New York Ethical Society a few years ago in which, as I recall, I said that their vision of society is also mine, for without ethical culture there is no salvation for humanity. I truly believe this.

—I am quite certain that my reticence in supporting the further development of these miserable bombs has its roots in my feeling that otherwise I would be betraying the high values taught so vociferously at the School. Especially my repugnance with the hydrogen or H-bomb, with its destructive power of over one-thousand times the ones we dropped on Japan.

—Well, we both agree on the need to control atomic energy J.R. You worked so hard for years on committees devoted to civilian influence on this problem, but your left-wing past and your perceived opposition to the building of this so-called super-bomb made paranoid right-wingers in political positions of power suspicious of your full patriotism – even scientists such as Teller. Ah, what more do they want? Without you this country would not have had the bombs to drop on Japan in 1945, which ended the war.

—Oh Albert, do not over estimate my importance at Los Alamos. Who knows what would have happened with another director? Indeed, it may have been better if I had not taken part in this gargantuan enterprise.

—Um, I have always detected in you, since the war, a sense of remorse or culpability over the egregious loss of life in Hiroshima and Nagasaki. I certainly have guilt feeling about my letter to Roosevelt warning him of the possibility of the Germans making a bomb with their knowledge of the physics of nuclear energy. How was I to know that, in the end, the bomb would be used on Japan instead? In 1946, I bought hundreds of copies of John Hersey's stirring novel, *Hiroshima*, and gave them to friends and acquaintances. I probably was feeling some shame over my role, even though I was not part of the Manhattan project that you ran. Remember, I was still a possible German spy to the Americans.

What a joke! By the way: is it true that you told President Truman you had blood on your hands?

—Well, I am now devoting much of my free time to lecturing and writing about what I see as the problems facing mankind since the war, because of the threat of nuclear warfare. We need – and you have written extensively about this – to control the proliferation of these heinous weapons. Perhaps even to make some accommodations with the Russians. I look forward to your manifesto with Russell that you told me about on your birthday.

—True, we agree on the control problem, but we disagree on the methodology or mechanism. I am convinced that only an international government with a world court will bring this to fruition. I have warned of a nuclear arms race unless all nuclear countries disarm. Otherwise, I see no end, except in nuclear oblivion. I said so on Eleanor Roosevelt's TV show a few years ago. But disarmament is an ominous word in this country, almost like communism. Whereas, you take a more so-called balanced approach. I see this as appeasement – in reality, just giving in.

—Well, Albert, you always took the direct approach, such as calling the AEC the Atomic Extermination Conspiracy after it took away my security clearance. I appreciate the thought. You are a most outspoken voice for disarmament.

—Yes, my big mouth. You know, I am sure I did Ben-Gurion a favor by rejecting the presidency of Israel a few years ago. Otherwise he would have had a big problem getting me to keep my mouth under control.

—I believe that you were given the offer out of obligation – after all, you are the most famous Jew in the world – but in his heart-of-hearts David Ben-Gurion was hoping you would say "No." Ah, speaking of your outspokenness: I will honestly tell you that I have been trying to keep the Institute out of politics. To preserve its so-called ivory tower insularity, as best I can. Of course, as an independent scientist and citizen, you may say whatever you like – as if I could muzzle you anyway.

—J.R., I am aware of your attempt to keep the Institute free of political partisanship. And I will not knowingly interfere with that, for I always speak as an individual, not as a member of the Institute. Incidentally, speaking of insularity, I wish to commend you in your effort to integrate the Arts and Science disciplines at the Institute. But sadly, it seems to be a failure. Mathematicians and historians barely speak to each other, let alone sit at the same lunch table. Isolationism at the Institute is severely ingrained. It was that way before you came in 1947, and it looks as if it will not be changed. In many ways, you are dealing with intellectual *prima donnas*. By the way: here we are, colleagues, ever since you became the Director of the Institute for Advanced Study. When did we meet earlier? I cannot remember.

—We had little contact before '47. We met a few times in California when you were on your annual sojourn to Caltech in Pasadena and I was teaching in Berkeley. We also met when I had a tour of the Institute in 1935, but I did not want a position here because I found the atmosphere too narcissistic and solipsistic. I believe that in a letter or postcard I called the place a madhouse. Ah, and now, here I am, directing these inmates. I do not recall much depth to our first conversations. To be frank, I thought that your quest at the time toward a unified field theory was a hopeless venture.

—What do you mean by "at the time?" You still do, I know.

—Well, yes, but in a different manner. I was sure, and said so, that your general relativity theory was a landmark in science, a work of genius, with its singular union of geometry and gravitation. Moreover, I found many of your relativity papers paralyzingly beautiful. But I also was skeptical about building anything onto the theory at the time, because of the lack of strong experimental support. Two experiments measuring very, very minuscule amounts, and a third still to be proven – that was not sufficient data to expend a lot of human energy, especially when there were so many astonishing breakthroughs in theory and experiment in quantum physics at the time.

—And you still feel that way, I know. I commend your recent hiring policy, with the shift in focus from pure mathematicians to mathematical physicists, but I see that those hired are always in quantum physics. You have not hired physicists who work in relativity, and you even have discouraged those who have tried to do so. You know something? I am not always "out of it," as you Americans say.

—Yes, uh, yes, to both points. But, Albert, I never questioned or quashed your work here in any way. I respect what you are doing. Indeed, I find it remarkable and breathtaking, and even inspiring, the way you have doggedly pursued this task of unifying gravity and electricity – there is a sense of grandeur about the entire enterprise. It is one of the great epic Ulysses-like scientific journeys of the mind: in the tradition of Kepler finding the orbit of Mars, or Newton discovering the law of gravity.

—Okay, okay, you need not go on.

—No, I genuinely mean that. Someday there may be sufficient reason for more work on your theory, after there is further empirical support. Perhaps, Albert, in the not too distant future, many physicists at this very Institute will be pursuing where you left off.

—Yes, maybe so. But there is a fundamental difference between you and me regarding the relationship between relativity and quantum physics. You view my unified quest as only having the goal of uniting gravity and electricity. I, however, have an entirely different vision. I have worked unflinchingly on the quest because I am convinced that by deriving a master unifying equation, it will follow that the fundamental equations of quantum physics will also be deduced. It is if the new unified general relativity theory will subsume quantum physics. In short, instead of quantum theory being a fundamental theory, relativity will be fundamental. The quantum rules will be derived *from* the relativity axioms, so to speak. And this will result in a complete quantum physics, not the incomplete version we have now.

—Well, yes, you are right. That is, I do *not* foresee that particular scenario. I do not foresee quantum physics being encompassed under relativity. At most, I see a combination or blending of them, equally, so-to-speak. But I still support your solitary pursuit, to the end, whatever that is. Ah, I just had a thought as you were speaking. Do you, perhaps, see a parallel between your unifying master equation for all of physics, and your idea of a world government and court unifying all the politics of the globe?

—Well, humm, it may seem to be a likely fantasy; that is, if you want to see no contradictions in all facets of my thinking. But fundamentally I see a flaw in the argument. Science is about the external world and its goal is objectivity. Politics, like ethics and morality, is about human behavior and as such is inherently subjective. As I have written many times: science is about what *is* and politics and ethics are about what *ought* to be. I see my politics as being independent of my science, but I know that others have looked, and will continue to look, for deeper connections in my ideas, all my ideas.

—It is best, I guess, to let these matters be settled by posterity. The agreeable part of this sort of thing is that we are usually deceased by the time this is all sorted out, and so we do not have to witness the egregious distortions of our life's history. In your case, Albert, it would be delight-ful if you completed the unification quest before you are gone.

—It will not come to pass. I have already said in my recent paper with Bruria Kaufman that it is probably my last word on the unified field theory, and I have no reason to doubt this. It will remain incomplete in my life. Um, anyway, what is the phonograph record you brought?

—Well, it is related to what we are talking about, in a way – a rather roundabout way, I suppose. It is another late quartet of Beethoven.

—Oh, another one of those avant-garde works he wrote in the latter years of his life? You know, I am not a fan of Beethoven. Too much emotion.

—Yes, yes, I know. Anything after 1800 is a degeneration of classical purity. And, you are correct: his late quartets were roundly rejected at the time as too erudite and forbidding. But now they are considered master-pieces.

—Ah ha, so you see Beethoven's late work as analogous to my uni-fied field theory. Yes?

—Yes, there is probably – well, better said, maybe – a parallel. Both were seen as too recondite for the times.

—So, that means that you think my theory – or at least the quest for it – will be accepted someday, so it will be a fruitful "epic journey" as you called it?

—Yes. Uh, and there may be other ways that you and Beethoven have parallel late works. I have been thinking about this recently; namely, I have been reflecting on the concept of what we call "late works" of creative men. Of course, we often do not know when this is until some-one dies.

—Well, I am not dead, yet, but surely what I am doing now is from the late period of my life, no matter how much longer I am here.

—Maybe, unless you complete your unified field theory, and then you will go on to something else.

—You are a real dreamer, J.R., yes you are. But, seriously, the con-cept of a late period in one's life is an interesting idea, as if it has some distinct characteristics, which would, in turn, be reflected in one's creative works – pictures, books, theories. Let me think: what characteristics? Humm, maturity, wisdom, serenity? A sense of resolution, yes?

—Perhaps, but it could go contrariwise: intransigence, restlessness, curmudgeonry, say, for not having solved or resolved some things.

—Or, a feeling of culmination, or summing up.

—Or, a repudiation of the past, and hence a fresh start.

—Oh, thus, it seems, J.R., that it could be anything. Hence, is there nothing special about a late period? Or at least, there are no common characteristics.

—Yet, intuitively, one has the impression that there is something unique about these late-in-life creations.

—Yes, and so perhaps I should reflect upon this some more – herein during, probably, my late period of life. Humm.

—Yes, please do so, Albert. And meanwhile, let us listen again to Beethoven, in *his* late period. Last time I introduced you to Quartets #12 and #13. Now we move further along, to #14. So, I wish to start with one movement, and tell me what you hear. It is the 6th movement, *adagio quasi un poco andante*, in g-sharp minor. This recording is by the Budapest String Quartet, who despite their name, have been in America since the 1940s. This was recorded for Columbia a few years ago, when they recorded all the Beethoven Quartets. This record has #14 & #15. … Here is #14. … Let me find the 6th movement.

—You know my aversion to modern music. I compare everything to Mozart. Incidentally, I am enjoying this record player the Institute gave me for my seventieth birthday. It is a marvelous gift. Beautiful music, right here in my room – and it sounds so real.

—Yes, I know. You thank me prodigiously every time you see me. Here is the movement. Open your ears, and mind, now.

—Ah, Albert, I see a twitch in your eyebrow, and a glint in your eye.

—Oh, that is lovely, somber, haunting, but familiar, too. Is it what I think? How did Beethoven know? It seems to be based on the Jewish Hymn *Kol Nidre* from the Yom Kippur service. Is it?

—Probably. It certainly sounds too similar to be merely serendipitous.

—As you know, by my teenage years I seldom visited a synagogue. But the few times I did go, I enjoyed the chanting. I once heard an exceptional *Shalom Aleichem* in California. But *Kol Nidre* has that deep association with the solemnity of *Yom Kippur*. So, this Beethoven movement has indeed captured me, and I look forward to hearing the rest the Quartet, and the flip side, too, as they say.

—Ah, ha, as I hoped the late Beethoven would.

—Yes, it began with the Mahler songs you gave me for my birthday last week. I played those Rüchert songs, and they are beautiful. I love those haunting melodies. It must be my age. They tap into something deep in my old noggin. I too am often world weary. Do you know that Bach wrote very late in his life a chorale called, *It is enough*? Sort of: "I've had it. Let me die." I am reading this book on Bach. Over there, please hand it.

Thank you. ... Ah, here, the lines: "Lord, if it pleases Thee/ I'll lay my burden down/ ... /My earthly cares no more/ It is enough/It is enough." Did you know that this chorale uses *all* the notes of the chromatic scale? That is what gives it its otherworldly expression, I believe; it never ultimately settles down on a tonic or a dominant. And Bach wrote this long before Wagner, no less.

—Oh yes, Albert, now I remember. I read about that. The chorale was used by Alban Berg in his *Violin Concerto*. For evident reasons, it appealed to him – since the chromaticism fit wholeheartedly into his avant-garde music, with the 12-tone technique, and such.

—Ah, yes. Berg, one of those *fin de siècle* Viennese composers breaking all the rules. J.R., it will be some time before I am willing to open my mind – and ears! – that far.

—I know, I know. For now, we will keep the spotlight on the late Beethoven Quartets. My aspiration was that the late quartets would open you to more than just Mozart.

—You already did so with Mahler. Ah, and from you, who cannot carry a tune.

—I know, Albert, but I also am deeply fond of music. I listen without singing. I feel delighted in having opened you to a wider range of music. Did I tell you? All these travails of the last few years have changed my outlook, exposing me to wider horizons. In an essay I am working on, I am stressing the need for modern western man to welcome the strange and peculiar, and to be gladdened to learn things that are novel and are not suspected – things that do not fit, that are different. Indeed, perhaps even alien. Here I am applying it to music, but I ultimately mean it in the larger even social and political contexts.

—Yes, yes, J.R., I look forward to reading that essay. And listening to more music, but, within some limits, of course.

—So, I have fulfilled my obligation for tonight. It is time to depart. You look tired and hungry. Having a nap before dinner?

—Probably, but before you go, I have been thinking about something scientific that I want to share with you before you leave. Back in the 1920s, when lecturing in Paris in 1922 specifically, I was confronted by singularities (or points of infinity) that came out of the mathematics of my general relativity theory for large objects, such as our sun; that is, if their radii shrank near zero, their gravity would increase to infinity. This was pointed out by the mathematician, Hadamard, who was at the meetings in Paris and spoke on this problem. I thought this put a major dent in my theory and I tried to argue against it having any physical reality. After all, why would a star, such as our sun, collapse? At the time, I called such an infinite entity the Hadamard catastrophe. I later reinforced my objection to this in a paper published around, I believe, 1939 that showed that such an idea would violate the relativity principle about nothing traveling faster than light. I now, however, recently learned that at about the same time, you published some papers with your students that showed stars larger than the sun *could* collapse using what we had learned from nuclear physics. Explicitly, that as a star uses up its fuel, such a collapse was indeed predicted. Thus, my general theory predicted that, for a collapsed star, the gravity would be infinite and therefore nothing could escape, not even light – so that the dead star would appear infinitely dark. A sort of pure black point in space would result. Do you remember this? I never knew this. I would like to pursue this, maybe?

—No, or yes, I remember it, but no, I have no interest in pursuing this any further. I think it is a dead-end topic.

—Oh?! I was hoping to pick up on this, for I have been having second thoughts about these infinite singularities, even though in my last appendix to my Princeton lectures I reiterated my objection to singularities. But now I am willing to admit that, in fact, maybe they are not catastrophic, and maybe we could, ah …

—I have no interest in the project. Those early papers are not worth developing further. A mistake is a mistake. Let it be.

—I have no one else to, uh, oh well, okay, J.R., let's drop the idea. Yes, let's, uh, I am getting tired. Oh, one more thing. Tonight, we are listening to the Mozart *Requiem* that you gave me. Do you want to join us?

—Thank you, I would love to, but I have other commitments. Yet, I do appreciate the offer. There are some Institute duties that I have to attend to this evening. I get minimal free time lately. Incidentally, that recording of Mozart is by Bruno Walter and the New York Philharmonic, with the Westminster Choir. Despite its name, the Choir also is fully American, directed by John Finlay Williamson, who is now settled right here in Princeton, New Jersey. So, please enjoy the experience: these new long-playing records are marvelous. Ah, I hear Miss Dukas coming up the stairs. ... Miss Dukas, thank you for the tea, and Margot's dainties were scrumptious. I look forward to the next tea party. Good-by.

—You are welcome, always welcome, Dr. Oppenheimer.

—Hope to see you soon, J.R.

—Ah, Dukas, let me relax by just gazing out my window.

—Enjoy the view Professor. We are preparing dinner downstairs.

Sigh.

J.R., humm. What I did *not* say to him was that I am very critical of his testifying and naming names before the House Committee. He should have refused and defied his government. But not J.R., too all-American. Why did he covet politics so much, wanting to be close to the power structure in Washington? I never understood this desire. I saw it in my friend Rathenau in Germany, and look what it got him – a barrage of bullets throughout his body.

Oh, Besso, did I forget you?

Ah, Albert, have you forgotten what you were taught? Remember your serious foray into traditional Judaism as a lad. You were taught about the old idea that the world's creation was never fully completed by God – that, so to speak, six-days were not enough, and hence the world is imperfect. As a result, it is up to us to complete the creation, to make it better than it is. It is man's duty to perfect the world, especially we Jews. Remember the Hebrew: *Tikkun olam*, meaning, repair the world. So, the creed of the Ethical Society about our duty to society was echoing a fundamental belief of a major strand of Judaism. Eh, Albert? What do you say?

Well, Michele, you make a good point. Indeed, Felix Adler, the 19th century founder of the Ethical movement, was the son of a Reform Rabbi, and he also studied to become a Rabbi. But Felix changed careers after reading the Kantian idea that moral judgments can be arrived at independently of theology. In other words, there is a secular path to moral truths, and he chose that path. But, of course, and accordingly, this does not negate the possibility of his Jewish roots still having an influence on his later thoughts. But – it just occurred to me – I do not think I ever thought about this idea of an imperfect world from a cosmological viewpoint. That is something to ponder someday. Um, a cosmological *tikkun olam*? Humm, have I been trying to repair the world with my theory of cosmology? I certainly repaired Newton's theory of gravity with my relativity theory. Yes? Um, so much to think about.

Sigh.

For now, I gaze out my wide window at the weather. The rain has begun again. Should I put the *Rüchert-Lieder* on the record player? It fits the mood. Temperature at 44-degrees. Thankfully, I am in this warm house. I could use a sweater, however.

Ah, speaking with J.R. about infinities just jogged my memory. "God is the Infinite Ground of Being." Who said that? Ah, yes, it was Tillich, the theologian Paul Tillich, who I met. Eh, philosopher-theologians like to capitalize words a lot, don't they? He made that pronouncement in response to my lecture in New York on a conference on science, philosophy, and religion, around 1940 or so. He too was a refugee from the Nazis. Hounded out of the country in 1933, lost his job, and his books too were burned by the thugs. I recently reread that essay. Where is it?

Shit, where is it?

Oh, here, yes, here. That's right: I put it within the pages of my book of essays, *Out of My Later Years,* published in (when?), oh, here, in 1950. Tillich liked what I said about what I called "the grandeur of reason incarnate in existence," which "in its profoundest depths, is inaccessible to man." I thought I made a good case for my theological position. I believe it was the culmination of many years of contemplating this theological problem, and I have not changed my feelings since. I even went so far as to write out the argument in an almost Spinoza-like propositional format. Humm, here it is, let's see what I said:

- For centuries, there has been a conflict between knowledge and belief.
- The development of science has supported the role of reason for discovering facts.
- But knowledge of what *is*, does not always lead to our understanding of what *should be.*
- Meaning in life is rooted in values, not facts; and this is not the domain of science.
- Religion has played a key role in the emotional life of the individual, and in this sense, it links up with the social life of man.
- Much of this social life is supported by belief, not reason, with a major part set by tradition.

- Thus, meaning is derived from tradition through our social life, especially in living with and helping others. (For me this is my cultural Jewish identification.)

- A truly religious person, therefore, is liberated from the bondage of his selfish desires and wishes. ("Of human bondage.")

- From all this I conclude that there is no inherent conflict between science and religion: what *is* and what *should be*, respectively. They are two different domains. (Of course, J.R. would quickly insert here the qualification that religion does not have a monopoly over human values. Witness what he was taught by his teachers at the Ethical school. And, I would agree.)

- So, or but, where does the concept of God fit into this framework?

- Historically God was the source of explaining all that is and all that happens. This anthropomorphic God replaced the polytheist gods of earlier times.

- Science has, for some thinkers, replaced God with human reason. But not me. I am not an atheist.

- I too am in awe of human reason. I certainly appreciate and exploit the scientific method, especially for making predictions. But it has its limits, such as for extremely complex systems: an everyday case is the weather – or, in general, the turbulence of continuous systems. For an example of the latter: there is still no exact equation for the motion of water moving around (say) a rock in a stream.

- Of course, from this it is clear that organic nature, an even more complex aggregate of systems, is less amenable to probing into an exact knowledge of its underlying order. Witness the human mind/brain.

- Nonetheless, I believe there is such an order, some of which I have found in my work on relativity for the material world. In my "striving after the rational unification of the manifold" of the physical world (my quest for a unified theory of all forces of nature), I have felt an "intense experience" that has moved me to a "profound reverence for the rationality made manifest in existence." This leads to an appreciation of "the grandeur of reason incarnate in existence," which, "in its profoundest depths, is inaccessible to man." This attitude, I believe, makes me religious "in the highest sense of the word."
- Furthermore, this liberates me from egocentric cravings, and accordingly it eschewed all anthropomorphic ideas of God – hence, I have dispensed with the concept of a personal God.

Ah, nicely said, humm, Spinoza and I: God is revealed in the order and harmony of all that exists in the universe. That is enough. No more, no less. So, Tillich's "God is the Infinite Ground of Being" – well, ah, that fits too.

Sigh.

So, Tillich liked my phrase, "the grandeur of reason incarnate in existence," which he also associated with an aesthetic feeling and an intellectual need in man. Yet it was not enough for him. Despite all his accolades for my argument, Tillich still wanted to salvage the idea of a *personal* God. Hard to give up, for sure. I agreed with him that we humans are fundamentally prone to a state of loneliness, anxiety, and despair. This is why most men need a personal God. Not only the idea, but more. Yet I still believe the concept is a remnant, a residue, of anthropomorphism, and therefore unnecessary. Tillich, however, was adamant: only a "person" can heal a person, he said, quoting the German philosopher Schelling. And this led Tillich to a "personal" God: the Godhead Person to the human person. I, however, clung to what I saw as Spinoza's God. And still do. The grandeur of reason incarnate in existence is enough for me. My loneliness and despair are tempered by the opulence of nature.

Indeed, the more I study nature the more I am aware of a spirit manifest in the laws of the universe, a spirit far superior to man, and which makes me feel humble. This is what I would call a religious feeling. Yes? Yes, I like this way of putting it, eh? And the opulence of nature? Ah, just look at that sky through my window, as the rain clouds part, letting the sun in. It has an orange-red tone as the sun is low in the west. What gives it that color? Humm, I like to do physics in my head, old physics problems that I formally taught during those years as a teacher, from (how long?): oh, 1909 to 1914, with occasional lecture courses during my years in Germany, as I recall. A short career as a formal university teacher. I was quite good, I believe. When word got out that I was leaving Zurich University, a dozen or more physics students sent a petition to the Department of Education, pleading that I be retained because I was an outstanding teacher who explained things clearly and had a good rapport with them. It made me feel (how should I say?), uh, fulfilled as a teacher. Ah, I recall once some neophyte teacher asking me for advice on how to be a good teacher, and I said that I had no positive advice, only negative. Namely: don't take yourself too seriously, and don't lose your sense of humor. Oh, if only my dictatorial German teachers had known that, um.

Ah, where was I?

Oh, yes, the color of the sky, yes, goes back to the age-old question: Why is the sky blue? Let's see: in the late-19th century it was known that blue light is scattered more than red light, and the particles in the air are responsible for the scattering toward the blue. Hence, the blue sky. But at sunset, we see the sun's light is coming directly toward our eyes, and since the blue light is scattered-out, we see the light as red or orange. Yet, this explanation was not sufficient, for we need to know more precisely how the particles did this, why each color was scattered differently. It was eventually understood that it came down to the molecules of nitrogen and oxygen in the air. In 1911, I calculated the formula for such scattering by these molecules and found it to be experimentally correct. Further calculations verified Avogadro's number. So, I too helped to explain further the colors of the sky. Ah, I have not thought about this for some time. Um.

Blue sky

orange sky

red sky

red

Reds

Communists

—This hearing will begin. Dr. Einstein, are you a US citizen?

—Yes. I became a citizen in 1940.

—What is your position at Princeton University?

—Well that is your first mistake, a common one made by the press I'm afraid, who do not know the difference between the University and the Institute for Advanced Study, which is an autonomous institution.

—Do you not teach courses at Princeton University?

—No, I am not on their faculty. I do, however, have a standing rule that students from the University may approach me any time to ask questions. The Institute is within walking distance of the University. Well, to be more exact, less than two miles.

—Dr. Einstein, are you a member of the Communist party or have you ever been a member of the Communist party?

—No, to both questions. But if I was, I would not be ashamed of it.

—Just answer the questions. Uh, were you a member of the Communist party when you lived in Germany?

—Logically speaking, a "No" answer to the previous question would entail a "No" to this one too, if I am not mistaken.

       laughter

—Do you know Dr. J. Robert Oppenheimer? And if so, uh, how long?

—Yes, I do. He is my superior (or boss, as you would say) at the Institute for Advanced Study. I first met him in the early 1930s.

—Is Dr. Oppenheimer a member of the Communist party, uh, or has he ever been a member of the Communist party?

—Why do you not ask him?

—Right now, I am asking you.

—I cannot answer what I do not know.

—Has Dr. Oppenheimer ever spoken to you about, uh, radical political ideas?

—Even though I have a generally disparaging opinion of politics and especially politicians, I often think, talk, and write about politics and social issues. So, yes, Dr. Oppenheimer and I often talk politics, from a wide range of views, and we do not always see eye-to-eye. Sometimes my views are more radical than his, I suppose, but it all depends upon what you mean by radical. Moreover, I suspect that you mean left-leaning radicalism, whereas I have more of a fear of right-leaning radicalism. Remember, I lived in Germany in the 1920s during the rise of the radical right. Nazi thugs assassinating people in the streets in cold blood. The murder of my good friend, Walther Rathenau, was a heartbreaking example. So, I am sensitive to any form of fascism that I detect – anywhere. Even here.

—Dr. Einstein. Did you write an essay titled "Why Socialism?" in the **Monthly Review***, an openly socialist magazine, in May of 1949?*

—Yes, I did.

—*Did you write these lines about the United States of America? I quote: "The economic anarchy of capitalist society as it exists today is, in my opinion, the real source of the evils in society. The members of the legislative bodies are selected by political parties, largely financed or otherwise influenced by private capitalists and private capitalists inevitably control, directly or indirectly, the main sources of information (press, radio, education). Therefore, I am convinced there is only **one** way to eliminate these grave evils, namely through the establishment of a socialist economy accompanied by an educational system which would be orientated toward social goals." Unquote. Did you write that Dr. Einstein?*

—*Yes. And I would add ...*

—*Just answer the questions. Uh, do you believe what you wrote?*

—*Did I not say, "in **my** opinion"? Who else might that **my** be?*

       laughter

—*Uh, don't get snippy with me.*

—*Well, when you ask a stupid question.*

       laughter

—*Dr. Einstein, did you ever visit Russia?*

—*No, never been there.*

—*Were you, uh, invited to come by the Russians?*

—*Yes, but I did not go.*

—*Why not? After all, it is a socialist state. Uh, your ideal.*

—*Not my ideal. My ideal is socialism within a democratic state, not a dictatorship, as Russia (or what they call the Soviet Union) is today. I believe in personal freedom as the cornerstone of any livable society.*

—*When was the offer, and why did they ask you to come? Uh, were you seen as a friend of Russia?*

—*It was around 1914, before the revolution, and it was about an eclipse of the sun taking place in St. Petersburg. You see, it is only during a solar eclipse that my general theory of relativity can be confirmed because the theory predicts that ...*

—Uh, we have heard about your esoteric theory. We are not interested in your science but, uh, in your politics.

—Well, in that case, I wish to inform you that within my written rejection of the offer to visit Russia, I pointed to the brutal persecution of my fellow Jews by Russian authorities.

—Did anyone from the Soviet government contact you since you moved here?

—Yes, last year. They wanted to give me a peace prize. I rejected the offer. That's all I needed: to be called a Bolshevik!

—Did, uh, anyone try to get you to join the Communist Party?

—No.

—Did you ever publish anything in Communist publications in this country?

—Not that I know of. What publications do you think are communist?

—What about that **Dialogue on the Two Chief World Systems?**

—That was Galileo in the 17th century, you fool. It is about the difference between an earth-centered universe and a sun-centered one.

—The difference is essentially that, according to our Holy Office in 1616, a sun-centered universe is heresy. Hence you, for presenting it in your book, are committing heresy, and may be called before this Inquisition.

—But I was presenting it, not as truth, but as just an alternative way of explaining the motions of the heavenly bodies as we see them from here on earth. We often just call this the phenomena; what we see. You see, there is more than one way to account for these motions; such as, even using the idea of a moving earth. Think about it: a day can be the time it takes the sun to go around the earth; or, since the earth is round, it could rotate once a day. Either way we get a day, eh?

—Our Holy Office declared the proposition of a central sun to be heresy. A moving earth, though, was declared to be "foolish and absurd in philosophy," and "erroneous in faith." Which is not necessarily heresy.

*—The difference could save my life, I suspect. Sounds trivial, but really not. We live in perilous times. That's why, I assume, Cardinal Bellarmine directed that warming to me: as I recall, it said not "to hold or defend the sun-centered system." But I told him I was doing neither in my book. I was just putting forth the **idea** of a moving earth as an alternative way of explaining the phenomena.*

—In that case, you should have nothing to fear, since Bellarmine makes a distinction between knowledge based on faith, with is truth, and knowledge from science, which is opinion. Unless, of course, someone in the Inquisition reads more into the argument in your book about a moving earth than you say you intended.

—I am getting uncomfortable with this discussion in a number of ways. How did we, er, I, get here? I was talking to the American HUAC about Communism. Now I am before the Catholic Inquisition, as Galileo. Wait, the Holy Office is irrelevant to me. I am a Jew.

—What, a Jew? Ah, as we suspected. A Jew and a Communist. So, according to the decree from the office of the Chief of Aryan Science, you will be relieved of all your positions in the Prussian Academy and the Institute in Berlin, and immediately transported to an internment camp for unbelievers.

—An unbeliever? An unbeliever in what?

—In Aryan physics, the true and pure physics of the folk.

—You must be kidding. You are not going to hand me that crap about Jewish Physics verses German Physics, are you?

—Your relativity theory has polluted the pure German scientific spirit.

*—What? Science is not about ideology, you fool. That is the purview of religion. There is no heresy in science. You need no inquisition. The realm of experimentation is where decisions are made as to the efficacy of any hypothesis. By introducing your foolish Aryan pseudo-science into real science, it is **you** who are polluting physics. As a consequence, you will destroy German science as long as you hold to these inane ideas. Already, Jewish and other scientists are emigrating to America, the UK, Canada, and elsewhere – anywhere but to stay in Germany. The result will be a devastating long-term lack of real science in this once top-notch culture.*

—No, the office of the Chief of Aryan Science will make sure that authentic Aryan science prevails, and keep Germany unsoiled.

—Who is this Chief? What are his credentials?

—None other than the Nobel laureate, Philipp Lenard, my master.

—Lenard? Well, um, no surprise. His early work greatly influenced me. His paper on the photoelectric effect was a work of beauty. But when we debated on my theory of relativity in 1920, he showed himself to be too much influenced by the endemic anti-Semitism. He let his ideology creep into his science, and it got the best of him. Now he has a highfalutin job that is grounded on worthless and impotent principles.

— Lenard will keep German science pure, as Hitler makes Germany great again. Heil Hitler!

—Shit on Hitler, and shit on Lenard. Heil Newton! Heil Faraday! Heil Maxwell! Heil ...

—Oh. What was that noise?! Uggg. Oy.

—Sorry, father. I am just collecting the cups and saucers and things from the afternoon tea, to take down to the kitchen. Why are you so agitated? Grumpy, yes? What's wrong?

—What's wrong? Oh, where to begin? What a dream. To start, I did not like my performance at the HUAC hearing.

—But what? You did not testify at HUAC? What are you talking about? They never called you, thank goodness.

—I mean in my dream, just now. I allowed those fools to kowtow me into answering their inane questions. What is wrong with me?

—Father, it was a dream for God's sake. Not real. Why be upset with a dream, good grief. Sometimes you are such a …

—No, dreams come from your unconscious, and they are about what you are feeling, very deeply.

—Well, let me tell the world that I heard it right here: Dr. Einstein spouting Dr. Freud, and you the great skeptic of psychoanalysis. What was that you once told me? – that Freud was …

—No, no. Despite my deep reservations about psychoanalysis, I still think that Freud's theory of the mind contains a profound truth about our behavior. What I did in this dream at the HAUC hearing is very disturbing, for it goes against all I have said to others who have had to testify. Remember that teacher from Brooklyn? – ah, Mr. Frauenglass, who was called before one of their witch-hunting committees, and he wrote me asking what to do. I told him not to cooperate with them; to refuse to testify, even to be prepared to go to jail and face economic ruin in the interest of freedom in his country. I called it an inquisition that violates the Constitution. Well, that was easy for me to say. So, when I am called, what do *I* do? I play their game and answer their stupid questions. Lord help me.

—It was dream, d-r-e-a-m, father. It did not happen, get over it. But I think I know why you are so distressed. Dr. Nathan told me that after your letter to Mr. Frauenglass was made public, you remarked to him that you were worried about being sent to jail. Did you truly feel it could happen?

—Yes, the present paranoia is profound and dangerous. In fact, I truly believe that this witch-hunting by politicians is more dangerous to this country than even a few communists in the government.

—Yes, it is upsetting to live here with Hoover and the Un-American Activities Committee intimidating good citizens, especially after all we went through in Germany. It reminds me of Galileo before the Catholic Inquisition; indeed, Father, you have called these hearing an American Inquisition. Didn't you?

—Ah, yes, Galileo. You know, in the second part of the dream I was indeed Galileo himself (or whatever) before the Catholic Church. Oh, I owe so much to him for the idea of inertia. But, you know something? I have often thought about his dispute with his Church, and the way he rather knowingly walked right into it; and for this, I think, Galileo was being terribly foolish. He knew he would be going into a den of lions, and that he could not win. Why did he do it? It baffles me. Well, I would do it for political causes but not scientific ones, because in science ultimately the truth will prevail. Social justice needs to be fought for, scientific truths do not. So, Galileo was acting in a foolish way, like a daft Don Quixote mounting his horse and battling unwinnable conflicts.

—I never thought of it that way, father. Although some political battles are unwinnable too, unfortunately. Yet, I would hope that we would be strong enough not to give into tyranny, for example. Yes, father?

—Yes. And in the last part of the dream, right before you woke me, I was back in Nazi Germany being grilled by some idiot. Which reminds me. Margot, I have been rereading your ex-husband's biography of me and I am curious about the events in Berlin in 1933 after the Nazis had emptied my bank account and then came looking for me in our apartment. Dimitri says that when he heard of the raid, he phoned you, directing you to take my important things to the French embassy. Did you do that?

— I do not know. I was so traumatized by those events that most of it has been wiped clean from my mind.

—Well, therefore, you may be shocked to know that he says that you were brave and courageous and remained calm throughout the ordeal.

—I find that hard to believe, since, well, you know me.

—Yes, I instead picture you hiding under a table or behind a couch.

—Me, too. I also do not recall reading that in Dimitri's book. Did I even read it? Since there was so much controversy about the book, and Helen kept bad-mouthing it as unreliable. Yet she did also concede to me that many things *were* true.

— Well, as I recall, Ilsa's husband, Rudolf Kayser, once told me Ilsa was there when the Nazis first came and she was scared out of her wits. So, she took a chance and had my papers sent to the French embassy so they could be shipped to America by diplomatic pouch. When the Nazis came again, taking books, paintings, rugs, and other things, the papers were gone.

—Father, why are you thinking about this now?

—I guess I am curious as to how and what future historians are going to know events in my life, although I usually do not care about such things. Anyway, I recently have been thinking a lot about the past, and for some reason, focused on the raid of our apartment in Berlin. You know, I suppose this is a case of my sons-in-law each trying to take credit for saving my papers and other documents. I need to ask Kayser about this the next time he stops by. And anyway, I was always leery about Dimitri, as you know. I did not like him much, and I question some of what he says about me in his book, which I too would call generally unreliable. Nonetheless, I would very much like to believe that his account of this incident is true. Stressful times can bring out the best (as well as the worst) in some of us, and I can conceive of your heroism – because you are, at the core, a most moral and honest human being. Your erased memory may be a subconscious mechanism for preserving your humility regarding this heroic event.

—I would like to believe that, father. For now, however, those dark days in Berlin have been expunged from my mind. But it would be nice to be a hero.

—Well, maybe it is true. Indeed, since the Nazis probably made several raids to our apartment, both accounts may contain a grain of truth.

—But surely only one of us was responsible for sending your papers to the French embassy. And I have no reason to doubt that my late, affectionate sister, Ilsa, was a hero. It is comforting enough to know that one of us was, and I do not care which one.

—That's good enough for me now too. In the long run, future historians will have to try to sort out the details. Humm, maybe Dukas knows about the raids. I seem to recall that she said something about being there once when the Nazis came. We'll ask her later. Oh, incidentally, there is one incidence at the time mentioned by Marianoff that I found rather humorous, in a dark way. When the Nazis raided our country cottage they were looking for weapons, but all they could come up with was a bread-knife. My weapon of mass destruction – if you ever saw me trying to slice evenly a fresh loaf of bread, eh?

—Yes, father, I know. Being able to find some humor in all this keeps us sane, I suppose.

—Speaking of Freud.

—We were, father? Um, are you changing the subject?

—Ah, yes and no. He was mentioned before, and when chatting with J.R., I thought of something else. Did I ever tell you about my correspondence with Freud on war?

—Well, there is that book over there on the shelf, *Why War?*

—So, sit down and let me tell you. Um, I met Freud on a few occasions and we corresponded thereafter. Nothing profound in the letters, as

I recall. Mundane stuff, birthday greetings and such. Except for the correspondence on war. It was I who initiated the dialogue on the topic. I was on the Council for International Cooperation of the League of Nations. The *international* facet of their work appealed to me, of course. I was asked to choose a subject and a correspondent for a series of books on current problems. I picked the topic: the causes of war and violence. And so, I wrote to Freud, another famous Jew at the time. He bit at my bait. His reply was a brilliant essay on the human factors that are grounded in war and aggression. Um, as you know, I have been a skeptic of psychoanalysis, but his work in social philosophy is an important contribution to a complex and thorny subject. Our exchange began in the summer of 1932, I believe, with my open letter to him. In it I first put forth my idea of the need for an international court that would have supreme power. Only with such an institution could future wars be prevented. I was still reeling from the bloodbath of the Great War. Freud agreed in his reply, and, as I recall, he added the idea of a second essential component – an international armed force to assert the military power required to keep the peace. Freud was particularly cognizant of man's destructive instinct. I was hopeful that something positive would come from his essay, and I spoke, as I recall, of it as planting a seed for some social change to arise. The little book appeared early in 1933, with a few thousand copies in German and English. It could have been an auspicious timing, for Hitler had just created his dictatorship and a serious essay on preventing war was just what society needed. But the minds of men already were polluted by demagoguery. Books by Freud and I were being publicly burned in bonfires. The cheering crowds were in no mood to contemplate peace. Freud put a positive twist to it by sarcastically saying that at least mankind had made some progress since the Middle Ages: the Nazis only burned his books, not him. By then I was in exile in America. Few read our little book, *Why War?* No one mentions it anymore.

—How interesting. I did not know. Let me take the book to my room and have a look tonight. Of course, Freud's little joke is not very funny in light what did ultimately happen – when the Nazis did incinerate people. Oh, look. Mr. Buchanan is hanging the birdhouse again on a tree.

—Ah, he sees me and, ha, he is orientating the birdhouse so the hole is facing my window, for me to view the birds darting in and out. If, in fact, any birds occupy the blue house. Hopefully a pair will find it.

—Oh, father, by the way. When Mr. Buchanan was cleaning up the ceiling this morning, he saw that I had ingredients out to make a bread. He told me that he had a wonderful recipe for Jewish egg bread that I may like. His mother got it from a family she once worked for, who made it every Friday evening before the Sabbath. I said I was delighted and honored to get his mother's special challah recipe. He often makes it for his family, so the recipe was in his head, and so he wrote it out for me. It involves, of course, eggs – and also brown sugar, honey, and lemon juice. I made it and we will be having it for dinner tonight, even though it is a Monday.

—How nice. I'm looking forward to fresh egg bread, it has been a long time since I had some. And I assume it will accompany the beef *à la* ceiling.

—Well, yes. But you are not funny. There was enough stew remaining in the pot for us, especially since it will be supplemented with a nice egg bread to sop up all the gravy that also remained in the pot. Father, you should be more patient with me, as I learn to use this new gadget. It makes delicious dishes, as you will see. I just have to know how to adjust that little jiggling thing.

—Ah, yes, that little jiggling thing. Humm, reminds me of a joke. There once was a naked man, who …

—No! Father, no! No more crude remarks. Remember? What would mother think? She tried to cure you of this repugnant behavior. So, stop.

Get over it! Oh, look, it's almost 5:45. The United Nations news broad-cast will be starting soon.

—Yes, of course, I listen to it every day. What will be the troubles of the world today?

—So, let me turn on the radio for you.

— I'll be down for dinner after the news. Oh, don't forget to give Mr. Buchanan his ice cream before he leaves.

♫ … and don't forget to buy your Pep-so-dent toothpaste, to-o-o-day! ♫ We now turn to

—Oops, wrong station. Umm, here goes, father.

… and this is United Nations radio, broadcasting the nightly news from the four corners of the world. Tonight, we begin in the Mediterranean where Archbishop Makerios of Cyprus announces his desire that Cyprus join Greece. This idea was immediately rejected by Turkey, who vehemently opposes any union of Cyprus and Greece. Meanwhile, the foreign minister of …

4. Evening

"If I were not a physicist, I would probably be a musician. I often think in music. I live my daydreams in music." —Einstein, 1929

Ugh, what's that noise? Woke me up. Oh, Margot is chipping away on one of her little statues. Well, at least my hearing is still sharp. Ah, an after-dinner nap in my cozy chair. I feel rested. Don't remember the dream; strange, I usually remember them clearly. Umm, burping some of that beef stew. Yes, she was right, the pressure cooker certainly does make a quite tasty stew. Ah, and that bread was delicious. Reminded me of some old challahs as a child in Munich. Who made those breads? Long ago: must have been a grandmother.

—Oh father. Did I wake you with my hammer and chisel? Sorry. I am still working on that little wooden statue of a grieving peasant woman. Oh, the phone is ringing. I hear Helen talking to someone, humm. She is coming up the stairs.

—That was Mr. Buchanan on the phone. He must cancel his work here for the next few days. His mother just died.

—Oh dear, so sorry. Ah, he was just talking to me about her this afternoon, and, of course, Margot made that wonderful bread.

—Margot, you and I will now bake an angel food cake for the funeral, and so, Professor, you must listen to Mozart by yourself tonight. ... Here, I will put on the record, and you will have to flip it over. Each side is about twenty minutes, so the entire *Requiem* fits onto one record. Are you comfortable?

—Much so, yes. Ah, maestro, wave your baton. Uh, okay, Dukas, drop the needle.

Requiem aeternam dona eis, Domine
Grant them eternal rest, Lord

Eternal rest, resting forever, what does that mean? How long is forever? Will my legacy last forever? Everyone still venerates Newton. Even Archimedes, who lived during the ancient Roman Empire, is deeply revered. We will never forget Pythagoras, around the 6th century BC, I believe. Who was before that? Who knows? No names. But Pythagoras will be immortal in memory as long as humans inhabit this universe. He not only gave us the genesis of geometry (triangles and such) but all of Western music, as well. For he discovered that the harmonious sounds produced by simultaneously vibrating strings – um, think of a lute or a lyre; okay, in modern terms, a piano or a harp – well, there is a simple mathematical order based on ratios involving only four whole numbers: 1, 2, 3, 4. He saw these as the foundation of all numbers, since $1 + 2 + 3 + 4 = 10$, and all other numbers cycle over this base of 10, namely 20, 30, … 100, etc. The resulting ratios that appeared in musical sound were: 1/2, 2/3, 3/4. In later terminology, they were called the octave, the perfect fifth, and the fourth. On, say, a piano, if I simultaneously strike **C** and the next **C** (up or down, one octave), then the frequencies of the two vibrating strings have a 1 to 2 ratio. For a **C** and up to **G** the ratio is 2 to 3 (the perfect fifth). For a **C** and up to **F** it is 3 to 4 (the fourth). For Pythagoras, these were the only accepted harmonies. The rest were deemed dissonant. It was true then, and still is today: these three sounds have a deeply harmonious resonance for all humans. If I were downstairs in my music room, I could strike these simultaneous notes on my Bechstein grand piano, rescued from Nazi Germany. Ah, but as music evolved over the many centuries after the Greeks, other harmonies were added, especially during the baroque era, from about the late-16th to the late-18th centuries. Specifically, the third (**C** and up to **E**) and the sixth (**C** and up to **A**) were added as sounding harmonious.

Ah, Albert, you know that this is not quite so. What about tempering that emerged in the Baroque era? No longer were the perfect numbers the bases of harmony. Right?

Yes, Michele, sure, tempering came into the picture, and therefore all instruments were not tuned *exactly* to the perfect whole number ratios. This happened because, with the rise of polyphony in music in the Renaissance, the instruments needed to stay in tune in more than one key, and this forced a change in tuning such that there was a slight departure from the *exact* numerical ratios, such as **1** to **2**. This was called tempering. Pythagoras may have turned over in his grave, but the method was necessary. J. S. Bach made an important contribution to this tempering idea: think of his *Well-Tempered Keyboard* – note the title? – forty-eight pieces in all possible keys; he wanted to prove that his tuning method truly worked, and in *all* keys. Just listen! Furthermore, over the years, others ratios that were previously deemed as dissonant were gradually accepted as harmonious. Today, since the late-19th century, further ventures toward extending the range of harmony continues, with varying degrees of success. Um, J.R. is trying to get my sensibility to adapt to this transformation. But I resist, as my sentiment is rooted strongly in earlier times: think, Mozart. Ah, this beautiful *Requiem*. Humm, it may not be an accident that Spinoza lived during the Baroque era. Remember that not only my scientific outlook but my religious viewpoint too is based upon Spinoza's affirmation that God "reveals himself in the harmony of all that exists." This harmony, not unlike that put forth by Pythagoras about 2½ millennia ago, I found in the mathematical structure of the universe. Perhaps Spinoza had music in mind too, when he spoke of harmony. Um, maybe, maybe so.

But, Albert, that was later in your career. You had a different attitude toward math when I met you. You even cut Minkowski's math class, you fool. No wonder he called you a lazy dog.

Michele, you are right. Math for me was just a technique or tool for doing physics, not an end itself. In my work in the 1900s, I saw algebra and calculus as sufficient for solving physics problems. Yet I found in the 1910s that so-called empty space was not just empty (a no-thing) which was filled with bits of matter, but that space itself had a structure that could account for gravity and maybe even electricity, the only two known forces in nature at the time. So-called empty space was *not* a nothing. Ah, yes, just like silence in speech or in a piece of music, which, as I realized this afternoon, are also not nothing. In the same way space is a thing in my relativity theory – like space in a poem. Having come to this conclusion, I then needed to find a mathematical formulation that could deal with this malleable, bendable, warpable, curvable, space – and for that I had to learn the new and recently invented type of math called non-Euclidean geometry, along with the corresponding tensor-calculus. Who knew that God could be so subtle? It was a revelation for me. Up until then I always believed that the scientific enterprise was at the core a careful balance between creative ideas and the need to test them in the experimental world. I still do, but I also experienced a further tantalizing conceptual shift by the 1920s. Geez, as you remind me Besso, I did cut most of my math classes at the Poly, to the exasperation of my teachers. Yes, Minkowski did call me a lazy dog. Well, I believed that math was the servant of physics, a means to quantifying the law-like features of the world. Also, mathematicians seemed to see math as an end in itself, whereas I refused to go along with them. When around 1908 Minkowski took my early relativity theory and put it into a 4-dimensional space, I said, in exasperation, that now even *I* did not understand my own theory. Nonetheless, a few years later I rescinded; he was right. Moreover, I had to go beyond his just 4-dimensional flat Euclidean space, since I was compelled to delve into a 4-dimensional warped space of non-Euclidean geometry, using tensor-calculus in order to solve the problem I had set for myself. Sadly, this lazy dog was never able personally to acknowledge my change of heart, since Minkowski died shortly after his now-classic article was published. By the 1920s I was humming a different tune about the role of mathematics in physics. I realized that math itself was an expression of the creative act, especially as I grappled with trying to unite gravity with electricity; in essence, this is my still unfinished unified field theory.

Indeed, Albert. Let me remind you – in fact, quote – what you said in a lecture at Oxford University in 1933. You affirmed that "the creative principle resides in mathematics. In a certain sense, therefore, I hold it true that pure thought can grasp reality, as the ancients dreamed." What an incredible thing for a physicist to say, Albert, huh?

Ah yes, what a radical departure from my previous thoughts on this. I still remember the unambiguous phrasing. This attitude is surely analogous to what Pythagoras was saying. Indeed, in the 17th century, the great astronomer, Johannes Kepler, thought he found various ratios in the mathematics underlying the motions of the planets, which he then correlated with some the musical ratios used in Baroque music. This was a variation of an ancient idea called "the music of the heavens" – the idea that the motions of the heavenly bodies produced musical sounds to be heard by heavenly beings (and perhaps some earthly ones too, who can hear them). The scheme was attributed to, not surprisingly, Pythagoras. Ah, notice how close my thinking is to Kepler's. You know, sometimes I think that if I were not a physicist, I would probably be a musician. I often think in music. Humm, I live my daydreams in music.

But Albert, in many ways you **were** a musician. You often spoke of your theory in aesthetic terms. There was not much difference between your statements on physics and someone speaking about an oil painting or a concerto. You spoke of the cosmological constant as gravely detrimental to the formal beauty of your theory. In talking about your theories, you emphasized the role of symmetry, simplicity, consistency, clarity, purity, balance – listen to your language, it is the rhetoric of art. And, of course, harmony: all exuding an air of aestheticism.

So, again, what did I say at Oxford? That through mathematics "pure thought may grasp reality, as the ancients dreamed." What an idea: what a quest. Grasping reality through pure thought. And so, I am still grasp, grasp, grasping, yes, I still am – ah, but the reality of the unified theory is slip, slip, slipping away, away …

Liber scriptus proferetur,
In quo totum continetur
A book, written in, will be brought forth,
in which is contained everything that is

Ah, yes, everything. So, my theory of everything is incomplete. So much for that quest of over thirty years. But there was another quest, started around 1925, when the quantum theory that I helped launch

150

around 1905 morphed into the quantum mechanics of present day, with its aura of almost mysticism around uncertainty, indeterminism, probability, and the absurd idea the world does not exist unless we perceive it. I have been fighting my almost sometimes one-man campaign against this incomplete theory all these years – and with little success, since quantum physics is so entrenched in the textbooks and curricula of most institutes of higher education. For this I am increasingly seen as being an old curmudgeon fighting a losing battle, and accordingly being called a fool. A fossil from the past. An old relic. But this portrait of me is only painted by the physicists, my colleagues. On the other hand, the general public views me as the epitome of the theoretical physicist, the genius scientist, still plugging away at uncovering the secrets of the universe – at least among those in the public who are enamored with science. They are oblivious to my rebuked status among my peers. Of course, the public also has a very limited understanding of what I did, or still do. They invariably refer to me as a nuclear physicist. Einstein: the nuclear physicist. Journalists, radio commentators, they all love the phrase "nuclear physicist." It is all the rage today. Nu-cle-ar phy-si-cist, has a poetic ring.

Nuclear physicist, nuclear physicist
Algebra?: we insist; not to be missed
Calculus?: don't resist; you must persist
Otherwise?: No physicist. No, no, physicist
No nuclear physicist, physicist, physicist

The other day I heard an announcer mispronounce nu-cle-ar as nuc-u-lar. And the next person, in making a comment, then did the same. Will they start a trend? What they do not know is that this designation of me as a nuc-u-lar physicist, or whatever, is completely wrong. I am not a nuclear physicist, nor have I even been one. In fact, I did not publish even

David R. Topper

one paper on the subject. This major branch of physics, started in this century with the discovery of the nucleus of the atom by Rutherford around (I believe) 1910ish, developed with no contribution at all from me. I was much too busy with relativity and quantum physics. I got as far as the atom, but never into its nucleus at the center.

Oh, Albert, glad to see you still occasionally pass the time by writing little doggerel verses. No, you were not a nuclear physicist. Yet, how about that cover of **Time** magazine on July 1, 1946, depicting you with a mushroom cloud behind your head, rather like an ominous halo, and **E = mc²** inscribed within the cloud. What a howler.

Yes, oh yes, I forgot about it. Of course, that little equation played a role in converting a smidgeon of matter into that enormous quantity of energy, destructive energy. But ironically, it was a transformation I did not believe could be achieved by human technology. When, for example, I was lecturing in Pittsburgh not long after we moved to America, a reporter asked me about the possibility of generating such energy. I said it was almost impossible to get real energy from a small amount of mass, and I gave him the metaphor that it was like trying to shoot birds in the dark in a land where few birds lived. Um, okay, a simile. I, of course, was dead wrong, once the nuclear chain reaction was discovered. Yet even then, and after a real chain reaction was produced – to which I made no contribution – there was a plethora of technological innovations independent of anything that I could do that were necessary to generate nuclear energy. Remember I am no engineer, despite my father's wishes. Moreover, because Hoover and others in the American government were suspicious of me as being a left-wing spy for communism, I was kept at arm's length from the goings-on at Los Alamos that J.R. directed. In the end, at most, I can be rightly called a theoretical physicist – and that's all. Enough? Yes, enough.

Inter oves locum praesta,
Et ab hoedis me sequestra
Place me among Thy sheep,
and separate me from the goats

Ah, yes, actually I am the goat. The rest of the physicists are the sheep. Then again, it all depends on how you interpret the symbolism of goats and sheep. Oops. The record stopped. Need to turn it over.

Umm. Yes, now, needle down.

Confutatis maledictis
When the damned are cast away

Damn. Where was I? Where, in my stream of consciousness? Or, maybe the stream of consciousness of Besso and me? Oh, lost it, ah, goats and sheep, where was I going? Ah, yes, quantum physics. Well, it all began around 1925. That's when I separated myself from the mainstream of quantum physicists. No one should forget that I put, so-to-speak, half of my scientific effort into that subject for about twenty years starting around 1905 with my quantum theory of light, which was the real first attempt to truly quantize the subatomic world. Previous quantum ideas, such as by Planck, were only mathematical manipulations to fit puzzling experimental data into a theoretical structure; he did not take seriously this quantum idea as a real physical theory, even though he introduced the word "quantum" into physics. Believe me, it is true: my quantum idea about light was rejected outright by almost everyone for almost all of those twenty years. I was the lone believer in real particles of light, the solitary believer – until experimental results in the 1920s could not be interpreted in any other way. It was not until around the mid-20s that even a name was given to these light-particles – photons, a term universal today. Yet, I do not disparage physicists for rejecting my idea. They had good reasons to hold onto the wave model of light that was worked out in the 19th century. Light truly does behave like a wave: it has frequencies of vibration, and especially exhibits the phenomenon of interference. How can particles interfere? It is still a puzzle. But now it is accepted that light, whatever it is, in reality, exhibits both particle and wave characteristics – the so-called wave-particle duality, an idea I (alone, as I recall) was pushing for as far back as around 1909. Another case of solitary me, eh? So, what is the post-1925 problem? Or what is *my* problem with it? Well, one way of looking at it is by thinking of my Danish friend Niels Bohr, who resisted my photon idea well into the '20s. But once the duality was a reality, he was immediately confronted with a paradox that he struggled to resolve. How could the subatomic world exhibit both wave and particle behavior? They were opposites.

How **do** you reconcile opposites? We talked about this again and again. Trying to get around the contradictions. Albert, admit it, we could not come up with a solution. We were stymied. And then Bohr put forth an answer.

Yes, Michele, a crazy answer. Working in Copenhagen with a small coterie of brilliant students, Bohr came up with what because known as the Copenhagen interpretation of quantum mechanics. Noting that the external world intrinsically had contradictory properties, he focused on the fact that these opposite properties were arrived at through different experimental means. On the one hand, an experiment that is looking for waves, finds waves in the subatomic world (such as interference); on the other hand, an experiment that is looking for particles, finds particles (of course, the photoelectric effect). Moreover, it is only through these experiments that we know anything about the subatomic world, since we have no direct perceptual access – unlike, say, my presently looking at this black circular phonograph record spinning and spinning at 33 1/3 rpm on my high-fidelity machine. Bohr leapt to the conclusion that therefore there was no real external world existing independently of human experiments – and accordingly, human perception. He said, in essence, we create the world by looking at it: in this case, by performing experiments. Yes, he truly said that: it was his way of resolving the paradox, having been exasperated with the contradictions within the phenomena. We create the world by performing experiments. He propagated this belief in lectures and writings and through his students – so much so that, in due course, it became scientific dogma. Today there are only a few physicists (along with me) who question this creed. But I told him it was nonsense, not unlike that of the 18th century Irish philosopher, George Berkeley, who used the Latin phrase, *esse est percipi*, which means: to be is to be perceived. I told Bohr that this idea meant that the moon would only exist if I look at it. How dumb is that? And yet I am called an old fossil.

Yes, I know Albert; you said it well in your biographical essay about your initial impetus to become a scientist around your early teenage years. Your flash of insight that "Beyond the self there is this huge world, which exists independently of human beings, and which stands before us like a great, eternal riddle, at least partially accessible to our inspection and thinking." But in your dream – when you were seemingly Galileo before the Inquisition – you were defending the position of science not pursing truth, but only accounting for phenomena, which was more like Bohr's position. Bellarmine, was looking for truth. So, you were taking on Bohr's position in your dispute with Bellarmine.

Michele, how do you know my dreams? Geez, is nothing private? Do I even have to defend what I do in my dreams? Well, maybe, yes, as I told Margot. Yet, I believe Galileo took that position to wiggle out of what he did. He, like me, believed in a real external world, and he also believed, unlike Bellarmine, that science can know that world. Science is not barred from truth – or as philosophers and theologians like to write it: Truth. Um, but Galileo's life was in danger. As I said, he never should have put himself into that den of lions. Yes, Michele, there is a real world existing independently of us – a basic tenet of my work, during all of my life. I will always hold that tenet. Always. Um, but: there is even more to my problem with the Copenhagen interpretation of quantum mechanics, because it also is about probability and determinism. Ah, ha, the "partially accessible" element of my flash of insight. Humm, more to rethink.

Lacrimosa dies ilia,
Qua resurget ex favilla,
Judicandus homo reus
Mournful that day,
when from the dust shall rise,
guilty man to be judged

I am persistently judged as being an old chump for my continued opposition to the contemporary interpretation of quantum mechanics. Yet, I feel no guilt, not at all. Indeed, I can't forget the fact that I started most of this. Yes, I did. I started this too, near the start of the century. Humm, let me think: even probability, indeterminism, and statistics? Well, yes, to statistics. From the start, my work on what became quantum theory involved my use of statistical methods to solve physics problems. The use of statistics began in the 17th century and came to fruition in the 19th century, even being applied, for example, to sociology (large collections of people). I applied it to problems involving the law of gases (large collections of molecules or atoms); I wrote a series of papers from around 1902-1904, even before the famous year of 1905. I guess you could say I was a pioneer in this statistical methodology, some of which I got from Boltzmann. Remember my telling Mileva about his magnificent book on gases? Well, I showed, for example, that my statistical method could be used to predict real fluctuations in nature, not just to account for things already known. Others who used statistics (for example, as in the kinetic theory of gases), wanted to show that the microscopic-statistical method led to the *same* results as the macroscopic approach (such as thermody-namics): that the two were, in short, compatible. Which, of course, was important for justifying the kinetic theory. But, also importantly, I showed my method to be even broader; that is, it was a more comprehen-sive theory, encompassing phenomena not accounted for by thermody-namics. It was thus a very powerful tool; for example, for explaining random fluctuations in nature, such as pollen grains suspended in liquids, which had *not* been understood before. I continued exploring this, and more, with my contributions to quantum physics right into the mid-1920s. It culminated in my work with the Bengali physicist, Satyendra Nath Bose, around 1924 and 1925, when we created a form of quantum statistics – what they now call Bose-Einstein statistics. We predicted a new state of matter for a gas near absolute zero, which is now called a Bose-Einstein condensate. No one has found it yet, but the experiments continue. Maybe someday, uh?

David R. Topper

Uh, Albert, I believe someday an experiment will find it, probably long after we are dead. Oh, yes, I am dead now. Humm. But, back to the 1920s. Here's the clincher: in and around 1925, just as statistics was becoming central to quantum physics for the rest of the theoretical physicists, you seemed to backtrack, or withdraw, or change your mind. Why Albert, why?

Well, Michele, frankly, I did not change at all, the others did. Think of it: they interpreted the statistical meaning of physics differently than I. Led on by my friend Bohr, they said that the statistical nature of the equations spoke to the essential structure of the reality underlying the subatomic world. There was, to them, no given predictable world; statistics was not about our limitations for grasping the totality of reality (as I believed, and still do), but was about the very *essence* of that world. That was why there was a wave-particle duality. For Bohr and company there are no real identifiable things in the subatomic world. Consider an analogy with the macro-world: we apply statistics to human behavior because we cannot predict the actions of individuals, whereas we can make predictions for large groups; that is why insurance companies make lots and lots of money. But no one would honestly say, therefore, that real individual people do not exist! But that was precisely what Bohr and company were saying. He said to me one time, directly: "There is no such thing as a quantum world." And he meant it as true. For him, all we have are our constructed descriptions of a reality that we can never know. It was the other side of the proposition that the world only exists when we look at it. But I did not agree, and still don't. I still see statistics in quantum physics as a method necessary because of the limitations of our experiments; think of experimental error. This is especially true when we probe into the subatomic world. That is why I was using statistical methods since around 1902. As I said before: reality is, at least, partially

158

accessible to us, since the act of probing itself places limitations on the veracity of what we extract as knowledge. It is about the act of *knowing* the world (our knowledge is statistical), not about the *world* itself (the world is statistical) – the latter is Bohr's interpretation, not mine. Why am I still flogging this dead horse so much? I obsess over it; yes, I do, for it has caused me much grief over these latter decades. I cannot let it go; I am still bickering with Bohr. Yes, bickering with Bohr. Ha, it never ends. I would not be surprised if Bohr, right now, is bickering with me on these matters. After I die, I suspect that he will still be bickering with me. Trust me on this. Well, I am not giving up. As I wrote in a letter long, long, ago when all was not going well for me in many ways: "God created the donkey and gave him a thick hide." That donkey was, and still is, me. Thick hide and all.

Ne absorbeat eas tartarus,
Ne cadant in obscurum
Neither let them fall into darkness,
nor the black abyss swallow them up

The year 1905 was quite a period in my life. In the order they were published, over several months, as I recall, I published these papers. *One*: the paper applying the quantum concept to light, what became a photon. It drew on the important experimental work of Philipp Lenard. Ah, yes, Lenard, whom Mileva took courses from when she left the Poly for a break from me, lecherous me. "Oh, that was really neat" – Lenard's "neat" lecture on the motion of molecules in a gas. *Two*: my PhD dissertation, in which I presented evidence supporting the existence of atoms, an idea that was *not* commonly held at the time. It was the most cited of all my publications for a decade or more. *Three*: a paper supporting the reality of molecules or atoms from what was called Brownian motion (that is, the random motion of tiny particles suspended in a liquid or gas). *Four*: my first paper presenting the theory of relativity. *Five*: my second paper on relativity, this one containing the equation $\mathbf{E = mc^2}$. Five papers in one year. In retrospect, it was a monumental accomplishment. Could such an achievement ever be denigrated?

Albert, have you forgotten? The anti-Semites denigrated your relativity theory in the 1920s, only to be surpassed by the Nazis in the 1930s – as Germany fell into darkness and was swallowed up into a black abyss. After the 1919 confirmation of your relativity theory by the solar eclipse experiment of the Royal Society of London, you were propelled into world fame, and in a short time the anti-Semites came out of the gutters. There was that rally in 1920 in (of all places) the auditorium of the Berlin Philharmonic by a right-wing political group – harmony replaced by cacophony. The "experts" accused you of plagiarism and propaganda. The plagiarism allegation was surely a red herring, for all scientific work is based on previous work. Real plagiarism involves deliberate copying from others. Even today no one has yet found you copying some or any sections of your writings from anyone else. Your work remains original. The carping about propaganda was strange, and undoubtedly exposed the blatant anti-Semitism of the entire episode. Since, supposedly, most newspapers that spoke on relativity were owned by Jews, the anti-Semites said that your theory should be dismissed. All of which shows the bizarre ends to which these fools groped to find something, anything, to attack in your theory. Grasping at straws. Ultimately, the outcome of this episode was their own propaganda: that there were two categories of physics in Germany: German Physics and Jewish Physics – an etymological dichotomy that the Nazis drew upon, so much so that they even set up a government position of Chief of Aryan Physics based on the racist pseudo-science of an Aryan race. Remember who held the post? None other than the "really neat" physicist, Philipp Lenard. Remember? How could you forget? Did it not come back to you in a dream today? Moreover, of all people, Lenard's attack on you used language that today could only be reflected back on him. He saw your work as an "alien spirit which appeared everywhere as a dark force." Today we turn Lenard's diatribe onto himself and the movement he represented. As the *Requiem* proclaimed: Neither let them fall into darkness, nor the black abyss swallow them up.

Requiem aeternam dona eis, Domine,
et lux perpetua luceat eis
Grant the dead eternal rest, O Lord,
and may perpetual light shine on them

Michele, old friend, you have reminded me of the bleak world I left in Germany, and which has haunted me ever since. You know, I have had nothing to do with that country ever since the last war and the cold-blooded murder of our people. I get invitations to join or rejoin various organizations and societies – but I outright reject them all. I will have nothing to do with Germany, as long as I live. Um, which probably is not very long.

Yes, these almost twenty-two years in America have been a respite for me, despite my misgivings about much that I do not agree with here, especially the recent rise of demagoguery by right-wingers. Humm, in many ways I find comfort in the final words of the *Requiem*: Grant eternal rest.

quia pius es
because Thou are merciful

Ah, this puts me into a serene mood: death, Mozart, what glorious music. Mozart, dead at age thirty-seven. I have already lived over twice that long. And Spinoza, only forty-four at his death, but I will surely not double *that*. I must thank J.R. again for this marvellous phonograph record.

Sigh.

So, Albert, let me leave you in possibly a lighter mood, with **my** stab at a doggerel verse:

> *nuclear physicist, nuclear physicist*
> *reads Bhagavad Gita*
> *dances Hava Nagila*
> *Nuclear physicist, nuclear physicist*
> *Sanskrit: Man's wit?*
> *Hebrew: Who knew?*
> *Nuclear physicist, nuclear physicist*

Ha, Michele, not much better than my efforts at verse. Yet, I believe J.R., the nuclear physicist, would be amused. We'll see. So, old friend, now departed, this reminds me: I need to write that letter. Let's see, ah, I hear Dukas coming up the stairs.

—So, Dukas, how did the baking of the cake go? I need to work on the missive to the Besso family, I must write something.

—The cake is done. You look rested after listening to Mozart. What about the letter? I am sure Besso's sister and son anticipate hearing from you. I will leave you alone, until you need to get your sleep.

—Dukas, can't I just, oh nothing, let it pass.

Sigh.

Yes, the solace of my study. Well, having revisited my life today – like a long episode on a couch (have I psychoanalysed myself?) – maybe, just maybe, I can now write the letter of condolence that I tried to start sometime this morning.

First, let me put that Ferrier-Rückert record on the phonograph. So, Mahler – put me in the mood.

Sigh.

I have become weary of the world,
the world thinks I am dead

Ah, yes.

Let me just start with some random thoughts, ideas, points I want to make.

Humm, Besso was not only content within his family, but he radiated his feelings to others around him.

His end was as harmonious as his whole life and, ~~even those~~ furthermore, the circle of those around him = ~~his family, his friends, his acquaintances~~. The gift of leading a harmonious life is rarely joined to such a keen intelligence.

Michele was so happy with Anna. How did he do it? One marriage to one woman, all those years. In contrast to me, never satisfied.

I live alone in my heaven, in my love, in my song.

But, I was in admiration of his ability to live happily with one woman all those years, in contrast to my failings in this human endeavor.

No, no good. Cross out the last sentence.

Not strong enough. I am too easy on myself. Although, I must say that I did triumphantly survive the Nazis and two wives.

I breathed a gentle fragrance

But what I admired most in him as a human being is that he

not only
managed to live for so many years in peace ~~with one woman and~~

but also in lasting ~~harmony~~ consonance with a woman - an

twice
undertaking in which I failed rather ~~pitifully~~ ~~miserably~~

disgracefully.

Yes, that's better. The word harmony, used twice, almost three times. Well it has been a concept central to my worldview, and is much on my mind recently. Um, Spinoza. Yet, *consonance*: ah, a better word. Has a strong musical connotation. Two notes sounding harmonious together –

like the Pythagorean ratios, 1/2, or 2/3, or 3/4. No wonder love poems often speak of two lovers in harmony. Michele and Anna. How did he, no, how did *they,* do it?

the gentle fragrance of love.

We met?

The ~~basis~~ foundation of our friendship was laid in our student years in Zurich, where we met regularly at musical evenings.

At midnight, I awoke, and looked up to the heavens.

And?

Later the Patent Office brought us together. The ~~many~~ conversations during our ~~walks~~ mutual ways home were of ~~important~~ unforgettable charm.

At midnight, I heeded the beat of my heart,

Michele's death. He beat me to it. What does it mean?

Now he has ~~departed~~ preceded me ^strange briefly from this world a little ahead of me. That signifies nothing. For we ^believing physicists, the distinction between past, present, and future is only ~~an~~ ^a stubbornly persistent illusion. In *a deterministic world all human thinking, feeling, and acting are not*

free but are just as causally bound as the stars in their motion.

In short, we all dance to a mysterious tune, intoned in the distance

by an invisible piper.

Um, no, no good. I don't like that last paragraph. Cross it all out!

At midnight, I yield all might into your hand,

Humm, let's try again.

at midnight!

Now he has preceded me briefly in bidding farewell to this strange world. That signifies nothing. For ~~believing~~ faithful physicists like us, the demarcation of past, present, and future has merely the significance of but a persistent illusion.

Ah yes, good. Enough. Now, a closing phrase, say.

A sincere thank you and sending you both all my best wishes,
Yours,
A. Einstein

Tomorrow: copy out the letter and have Dukas mail it off. The task of the day – accomplished. Only one page, but it took all day. Could not get started. What was the catalyst, Michele? Um.

Ah, now, I can slip next door into my bedroom and go to sleep. Before Dukas comes to tuck me in; oh, she can be so patronizing sometimes.

Ah, yes. My old bed, soft in spots, like me, but still functional to my liking. Like an old shoe. Relax. Okay, try to sleep, bed is comfortable, pillow just right, ahhh.

Albert, what is this gibberish you are putting in this letter to my family? What is this illusion that you speak of? Are you still going to harp on that determinism thing? And in a condolence letter, of all places? Yes, I know, determinism has been a constant in your work. Contrary to the apparent relativism of relativity, strict determinism remains central to your theory. Cause **A** produces effect **B**, which, in turn, is the cause of the effect **C**, etc. From **A** to **B** to **C**, in that, and only that, order. In your relativity theory, the times between these events may be different among different viewers, since time itself is not an absolute variable, but no one would see (say) **B** happening *after* **C**, or **A** *after* **B**. The sequence, **A** causes **B** causes **C** is still the same for *all* viewers, relativity or not. Unlike quantum physics, in relativity there is no uncertainty or non-determinism, as you know, Albert. And certainly, no time reversal. But you should also know that the underlying determinism of the physical world does not inevitably lead to reality being an illusion or to a lack of free will. What happens on the macro level is not completely determined by the micro level.

You know this Albert. Consider thermodynamics, where heat is the measurement of the motion of molecules. Heat is a macro entity. A molecule is a micro entity. But any *one* molecule has *no* heat. Heat is thus a meaningless entity at the micro level, yet it is a real entity on the macro level. Just because the question – What is the temperature of a molecule? – is meaningless, does not make temperature any less real for a body made up of many, many molecules. Everything at the macro level is not determined by the micro level. There are new *real* things at each higher level. So, we humans may have free will and our perceptions of the world may be real, no matter how strictly the underlying physical world is deterministic. Eh, Albert? Remember what you wrote in your *Why socialism?* essay: "Human beings are *not* condemned, because of their biological construction, to annihilate each other or to be at the mercy of a cruel self-inflicted fate." Well said, Albert, well said!

Humm, this is something to sleep on, no doubt. Michele, you still keep me on my toes, you old rascal.

Oh, Albert, one more thing from your old rascal. You mused about how I stayed content with just one woman my whole married life? Well, Albert it all comes down to three little words.

Really, Michele? Just "I love you"? That's it?

No, Albert, you fool, that's not it. The three little words are: "Lots of sex."

Ah, Michele, you rascal, you rogue. Who am I talking to? How does this work? Elsa was right: I do not know everything.

Sigh.

Ah, I was hoping to fall asleep easily after finally finishing that letter. Now Michele has stirred me up. Especially with his challenge to what I have written. Illusion, reality. Micro, macro. But I'm not going to change what I wrote in the letter. I want to believe that reality is an illusion. It makes facing death less disconcerting. Yet he is right about the free will issue. Which reminds me. So many of my thoughts today have brought me back to my past: my childhood, my obsession with Judaism in my pre-teen years, and the very orthodox worldview. That Yiddish word, *beshert*, a term denoting the idea of a world controlled completely by God. Nothing happens accidently. (Didn't Freud say there were no accidents?) How to translate *beshert*? Destiny, fatalism, everything preordained, there are no coincidences, nothing happens by chance, all has a purpose – as if the whole lot is a sort of set-up by God. Therefore: is my fidelity to a deterministic universe in my philosophical cosmology derived, in part, from the Jewish training of my youth? Humm. Ah, but Leibniz had this idea of a pre-ordained harmony of the universe. He famously called it the "best of all possible worlds." An idea ostensibly demolished by Voltaire in *Candide*. But Leibniz was not talking about human experience, this vale of tears. Like Spinoza, it was the physical universe that was his focus. Humm, Leibniz, another 17th-century thinker, also enamoured with harmony. Or, *beshert*? What was that quote from him about music that I recently read? Something about, uh, making music being the joy of a mind engaged in counting without being aware of the mathematics. Ah, Leibniz, I like that. Making music is a mind counting without being aware of the mathematics. What a genius he was, into so many fields of thought; argued with Newton over God's role in how the universe works. Humm, where am I going with this? I should be going back to sleep. Yes, well, time to close my eyes, and time to sleep? *Time*, again, I can't get away from it.

Sigh.

Maybe I can work backwards: start with death and see what it may infer about reality. How does the world appear when someone is dead? Being dead, um, is that a contradictory phrase? Being is existing; dead is, well, not existing. So, can you *be dead*? Departing this world, falling into, why falling? Some may say ascending, to heaven. But up and down are relative in relativity. Departing into the next world, a world? No, there is no other world, there is just nothingness. Where was I, say, seventy-seven years ago? Nothing? Yes, nothing.

   no thing
             no being
                   non-existence
                         no presence
                               perchance to

5. Late-night

> **"To one bent on age, death will come as a release. I feel this quite strongly now that I have grown old myself and have come to regard death like an old debt, at long last to be discharged. Still, instinctively one does everything possible to postpone the final settlement. Such is the game that Nature plays with us."**
>
> **— Einstein, February 5, 1955**

Oy, another storm. Wakes me up. In the middle of the night? What time is it? More rain. On and off, all day yesterday. Lugubrious atmosphere. Mirrors my temperament. Contemplating death episodically. Well, I finished the letter to the Besso family. Good, I feel better about that. Humm.

Sigh.

But I can't get back to sleep. Geez, I kept dozing off during the day, but now, when I *want* to sleep, I wake up, and, oh well. I may as well do something. I'll just slip next door, into my study, trying not to wake Miss Dukas in the other room.

Uh, turn on a dim light. Um, yes.

Ah, settle into my desk chair, and stare at my cluttered desk. The Bach book I am reading, here. Right there, my book of the Princeton lectures. Um, still waiting to see the latest edition (yes, it will be the last edition, I'm sure), with my final attempt at a unified field theory. Why has the Press not sent me this last edition? I wrote the final preface in December. Well, anyway: um, my desk. Bach here, physics there – music and mathematics. Mathematics and music, joint joys of my life. Twin delights.

Oh, Michele, why does mathematics intimidate so many people? Why does the sight of an equation turn them off? It would seem to me that a page of sheet music should be as impenetrable as a page of math for anyone not versed in either notation. Let me find a line in my Princeton Lectures book. I want a sentence that is straightforward for most of us familiar with advanced math. Ummm, …ah, here's one: "If, as in the special theory of relativity, we take the fourth co-ordinate as imaginary, this means that we must put $g_{\mu\nu} = -\delta_{\mu\nu} + \gamma_{\mu\nu}$, in which $\gamma_{\mu\nu}$ are so small compared to **1** that we can neglect the higher powers of the $\gamma_{\mu\nu}$ and their derivatives." No problem, eh Michele, once the terms are defined? But you know how that short sentence would fare in a book for the general reader. "An equation! Oh, the horror, the horror!" He would be stopped right in his tracks, and maybe even terminate any further perusal of the book as a whole – unless, perhaps it was put very near the end of the book, eh? Humm. Now, let me pick up the Bach book. Ummm, …here. Compare my sentence on relativity with the following analysis of the final ending of Bach's *St. John Passion*: "There is a minor-7th chord, with a chromatic **D**-flat, and an **A**-flat major triad, followed by a cadence that rests on a minor of a **III** chord." The average reader, not versed in musical notation, would, I surmise, just read over it and just continue onward – the way readers often skip over words they do not know the meaning of, but are too lazy to stop and look up. I believe that the musical terminology does not stop and jolt the general reader the way equations do. Why? I wish I knew. I probably never will know why, since I was never anxious about math. Do you agree, Michele?

Yes, Albert. But for an answer to a slightly different question, I am willing to make a stab at. It is this question: Is there a conceptual difference between musical and mathematical notations? I believe, yes, and in this way. The fact that a page of music is ultimately transformed into a sound that anyone can hear and enjoy constitutes a critical distinction. A dense page of mathematics, on the other hand, does not convert to any sensual entity; it remains an abstract enigma, knowable only to those who can read the hieroglyphics. At best, perhaps some novices many comprehend the math page in a minimal sense, if someone tries to explain the meaning of math in everyday terms. Nonetheless, the really marvellous thing about a page of music is that it can be heard – and that makes all the difference, I believe. I am sure of this, at least as a factor in the lack of intimidation by musical notation. I can imagine the reader saying: "Oh yes, those little flags turn into notes, notes that I can hear. Okay, I'm fine with that. But, on the math page, that long **S** squiggle (an integration symbol, you say?), so, what is that? What does that turn into?" What do you think, Albert?

Yes, you may be right. In fact, it brings to mind something that my friend Otto the economist once said about this. To get a student's attention to mathematics, just put a $ sign before every number, and all perplexity is dissipated. "Ah, yes: $98, I know what *that* is." True.

Ah.

What else is on my desk? Oh, that envelope of photographs that Margot and Dukas found among my mother's things after she died. Maybe it is time to go through some of these family heirlooms. What are these?

173

Humm, early family pictures, yes, those stiffly posed set-ups in a photographer's studio. Silly outfits we wore. Ha, Maja holding a parasol like a woman in a Japanese print. This was all-in-vogue at the time, late in the last century. An obsession with Japanese culture – foreign, exotic. The whole Oriental thing. Margot was recently talking to me about the Eastern influence on the Impressionist artists. After our trip to Japan, Elsa and I briefly fell under a similar Oriental spell. Oh, ah ha, look at *this*: my class-picture from my school in Munich, around 1889 or 1890 – I think? I was ten or eleven years old. Where am I? Umm, oh, here I am, front row, down in the lower right corner. The smallest lad in the front row. As I recall, definitely the smallest lad in the entire class. How many students? Five rows: 1, 2, 3, ah, … 52. A large class of 52 lads. Do I recognize anyone? Can I remember any names? Let's see, row by row: no, no, Heinz somebody, no, no, no, Steffen Fuchs, I think. No, no, no, Albrecht uh Koch maybe, no, no, Günther somebody, no, no, humm. Who else? Ah, Oscar Bauer, yes, um somebody Barth, or Junker, I believe? Oh, somebody Engel, I recall. I guess that is all. So, not too many lads were very memorable, it seems. But, ah, how interesting – they all stand at attention with frowns on their faces. Ha, this lad is stern; he is anxious; this one intimidated; others sulky or scared. No one appears happy or relaxed – no one, no one, except, except me! Oh look, I stand with my weight slightly shifted onto my right foot, my hands behind my back, and a cute, little, slightly impish smirk on my face. Am I the *only* one? Yes! Good Lord: I am the only lad vaguely smiling in the entire class-picture.

Sigh.

Humm, me alone, *only* me – the solitary lad with an impish smile. Ah, what to make of this? Ah, one smirky smile. The story of my life, summed up in one picture – a solitary smile.

Sigh.

Is it a visualization of my social attitude of being already out-of-sorts with the Germanic culture in my pre-teen years? Can some iota of the non-conformity of the rest of my life be read into this one picture from my childhood? Surely it could be tantalizing fodder for future historians looking into my life. If, indeed, anyone ever looks very carefully at this picture of me and my Munich class. I am so glad Margot and Dukas found this envelope. Did they not look at these pictures closely? I suspect not. Um, I am tempted to wake them up, but, oh no. I'll show them in the morning. Let me just sit down in my cozy chair, and relax.

Ahh. Well, it seems it took the one Jew in the class to break the rigid code of conformist behavior. Is this why a teacher once told my parents that my presence in the class induced a lack of respect for authority among the other students? Is my smirk saying that I know something that the teacher is trying to hide or suppress? Was I a little devil? Maybe, I cannot recall. Ah, I remember asking questions that sometimes the teachers could not answer. Those Germanic types could not handle this. Always needing to be in complete control. A militaristic atmosphere, with teachers acting like sergeants. Humm, this reminiscing about grade school is clearly not a nostalgic recollection. But, at least I can say that, from this class-picture, I was cute! Very cute.

Um, what happened to all these mainly nameless lads? Which ones became Nazis? Which ones worked at death camps? Who would have escorted me to a gas chamber? Or, even before that: which ones died in the Great War? Let's see, they would have been around thirty-five years old, and the military was still taking men up to forty-five as the war progressed. So, maybe, many of my co-students were of the so-called lost generation. These rigid German lads marching to their deaths with the same stern looks that, uh, uh ...

uh

       uh

             uh

Marching off to the Great War. Why am I in this trench? Like a rat on the ground, and yes with rats, all around us. Mud, rats, stench. I'm thirty-five years old? Why did I come back to Germany, when I left at fifteen? It was a mistake, a big mistake. Now they throw me in this trench. After all, I was not fit for service in the Swiss army. I flunked the physical test – they said I had flat feet and varicose veins. So, why am I, agggghhhhh, what was that blast?

Death all around me, am I going to die too? What if I die? 1914: I did not finish my relativity theory. Since 1905, I have been trying to extend the special theory to all motion, not just linear motion. Hoping this general theory of relativity will explain gravity, too. If I do not do it, who will? Without the general theory, there will be no new cosmology of a 4-dimensional universe, and no search for a unified field theory. Oh, well, I never did finish that, and probably never will.

More shells falling around me. Again, that was close. And another…

—What was that bang? It woke me. Ah, Dukas, what are you doing?

—Professor, what are *you* doing? Up this late? There is a storm outside, again. I could not sleep, so I was reading.

—Dukas, do you have to always wear those dumpy housecoats? Do you even sleep in them? **God, she is so matronly**.

—Professor, I do not complain about your attire, such as the socks you wear, so why are you mocking me?

—But I don't wear socks. So, ah, yes, I see. It was a joke. Ah, yes, ha. Why do you slip these by me? Why do I, oh well. I like your sense of humor. I do. After all these years, I guess we are like two old cronies. Anyway, I could not sleep so I came to sit in my study – and, of course, I dozed off. I was dreaming about being in the trenches in the Great War. Do you know that I was in one of those trenches?

—What? You were not in the First World War.

—Well, no, not in the war. But, sit down; let me tell you this story. Then we both can go back to bed. It was before Elsa hired you. In 1922, I recall, during a visit to Paris for a series of lectures and seminars on relativity. The animosity over the war still lingered, strongly too. There were many opposed to the visit, both among French and German scientists. I hesitated to go, but I was a friend of Rathenau, who was Germany's foreign minister at the time, and he convinced me it was important that I go to initiate a mending of the rift between the two countries.

—Yes, I know all about that professor. You should go to bed.

—Wait, let me finish this story. *Oy, she is so bossy.* You see, the French delegation met me at the Belgium border and provided an escort for me to Paris, since there were some threats made by French ultranationalists who were opposed to a German visitor. In the end, the trip went off without an incident, although some French scientists boycotted a reception for me. Near the end of the visit I was taken to eastern France to see some of the aftermath of the war. I was repulsed by viewing what was left of an entire village destroyed by German troops; all that remained was rubble. The actual carnage must have been dreadful. I also went into some of the trenches that have become memorials from the war. It was a moving experience, recalling the mud, gas, and fear that must have pervaded the place. Today all this is preserved for the tourists. Have you seen the movie version of Remarque's novel, *All Quiet on the Western Front?*

—Yes, professor. It portrayed well the futility of it all. It made me into a pacifist, that is until, naturally, the rise of Hitler. You too made such a modification or transformation.

—Yes, after Hitler for sure. But I was having misgivings long before 1933. After returning from Paris, there was a German-French friendship rally at the German Parliament in June, where I was met with much applause. But all that hoopla was short lived. A few weeks later Rathenau was assassinated. I thought: was I to be the next Jew assassinated by right-wing thugs? In fact, I started receiving death threats. Elsa and I had serious thoughts about leaving Germany. But we stayed, although it was a relief that, in a short time, we got away from Europe's troubles by making that long trip to the Far East. But, you know, in some ways it was a mistake for me to return to Germany in 1914 – to be almost immediately confronted with the Great War and the excessive German militarism that I detested, since it was one of the reasons I renounced my citizenship after I left the country as a teenager.

—Well, professor, it is a little late to second-guess this now.

—True, but still, it was difficult, with my colleagues in Berlin supporting the war, and with enthusiasm. Planck, who I had deep friendship with; Planck, who was a fine cellist, and with whom I played chamber music (he played piano and organ too); Planck, who introduced the word quantum into physics; Planck, who, like Haber, also signed that nationalistic manifesto. Do you know that Planck's son died in that war? And another son was executed by the Nazis for a plot against Hitler in 1944. What a sad personal life. His two daughters both died giving birth to their children. Only a son was left, a son from his second wife. His first wife died of tuberculosis, I believe. Ah, speaking of Haber: do you know that around 1934 Planck tried to keep Haber's memory alive by organizing a memorial to him, which hundreds of people attended? It was a rare act of defiance against the bullying Nazis.

—Yes, professor, I remember that. But why are you dwelling on all these woes of yesteryear. Moreover, it is the middle of the night and you need your sleep.

—Well, Planck came to mind while I was listening to the Mozart *Requiem*. I was free associating about my scientific creations over this past half-century. I think I covered almost everything of importance, I believe. Ah, what a scientific record: the range and the depth. Yes, my poor father would be proud. He worried so much about my stalled career. Ah, if he only knew?

—All this should give you solace. Enough, at least, to relax you now, and get some sleep.

—Yes, I think I can sleep now. Good night, again.

Humm, back into my bed. Ah, why was I dreaming of dying in the Great War? If I had died in that war, would the theory of relativity have been found by now? Maybe, and then, maybe not. Although it would eventually be found, I think. Yes, I am sure, as it expresses the laws of the natural world. But surely it would not be in the form that I produced. In the final analysis, textbooks always distill the essence from a theory such that it looks almost nothing like its original formulation. Um, yes, I fully realized this fact when, as a student at the Poly, I first came upon a copy of Newton's *Principia* in the library, and I sat down to read it – translated from the Latin, of course. Newton's masterpiece: the foundation of classical mechanics. But, upon entering the written text, I was stupefied. I had no comprehension of most of what Newton was saying. It was written in the strange 17th century language of physics. It was nothing like a modern textbook on what we call today Newtonian mechanics. There wasn't even the simple equation for force, mass, and acceleration: $\mathbf{F} = \mathbf{ma}$. I immediately realized that, contrariwise, if Newton came back from the dead, he would have no understanding of a textbook from today purporting to be on his science! They are *that* different: the original formulation of a theory and the later distillation of it in textbook-format are very much two different domains. So, I wonder what the theory of relativity would look like if I died in the war? There is no way to know. The same would be true with my unified field theory, but it looks as if I will not finish that, so this is a meaningless speculation. I will never know what the theory will ultimately be.

Humm, I recently read something about my search for a unified theory. Someone called it my unfinished symphony, an obvious reference to Schubert's *Eighth Symphony*. But after thinking about this, I disagree with the analogy. His symphony is not called "unfinished" because Franz died. In fact, he lived about six more years and wrote another symphony before he died. The *Eighth* is called unfinished because it only has two movements, not the customary three or usual four. I believe he thought that, with these two movements alone, he had put forth all of what he wanted to express in this piece. Why be forced into a convention – just to be conventional? I should know. Yes, Lord, I should know.

Humm, music, unfinished. Today is Bach's birthday. March 21st. Born, let me count, um, yes, 270 years ago. I am enjoying that book on his life and letters. His last work, which was, sadly, unfinished, is the masterpiece, *The Art of the Fugue*, published after he died in 1750. The fugue format is essentially an intricate weaving of several melodies into a harmonic whole, the most developed form of counterpoint. An initial thematic melody is repeated in several different pitches and weaved among other variations of the theme, finally coming back to the theme. The weaving is the counterpoint, one of the most beautiful expressions of harmony in all of music, anywhere, I believe. That is why Mozart was enamoured with it, and it appears throughout his work. He put a fugue in the last movement of his *Jupiter Symphony,* which I feel is one of his greatest works, perhaps the most perfect.

Oh, but, Bach. Yes, J.S.B. The fugue. In what would be the last fugue that he wrote, he introduced a melody based on four notes: **B**-flat - **A** - **C** - **B**-natural. In the German notation of the time, these notes would be written as **B-A-C-H** – his own name! In a fate of deep irony, Bach died without completing that self-referencing fugue. For this reason, the work is seldom played, since its ending is a stark and unexpected silence. In the middle of a phrase, no resolution, a sound left hanging. Um, another type of silence in music. The silence of absence, the absence of BACH. Bach, ends with melancholy, unfinished. My UFT, my unified field theory, never completed, an un-finished theory. Un-Finished Theory, a UFT! Ha.

I die, and no one picks up on the problem. Problem ignored: no one plays the BACH-Bach Fugue, unfinished and unplayed. Nobody searches for the UFT: it remains an un-finished and un-found theory UFT.

UFT
UFT
UFT

Am I flying, again? Flying? No, floating, oh, floating in my study. Looking around. Oh, there is my comfy chair, my familiar wicker waste-basket, and the large table from, ah, someone is walking around. Is it me? Hard to make out who it is from above. Well, he is not me, different hair. Not accustomed to seeing people from this viewpoint. Is this how God sees us? Why not from below, or some 4-dimensional non-directional sense? But God surely does not see us in this material sense, though eyes. The eyes of God are, of course, a metaphor. Anyway, I do not believe in this sort of God. So, where am I going with this, while someone is rummaging through my office? Ah, it is Besso. Head of thick, curly, and white hair with a full beard. Why not? Of course. Walking around in a strange colored robe. What does this mean? He is looking at the pictures on the wall – portraits of Newton, Faraday, Maxwell, my intellectual mentors. He stops at Maxwell.

Ah, Maxwell, late-19th century, formulated the fundamental equations that explained all electricity and magnetism in the universe. Much of my *first paper on relativity was based on Maxwell's work, from the first sentence, still seared in my brain: "It is well known that Maxwell's electrodynamics – as usually understood at present – when applied to moving bodies, leads to asymmetries that do not seem to be inherent in the phenomena." Listen to the aesthetic nature of the problem: asymmetries, a lack of proper order or harmony. Spinoza, Spinoza's God, my God. God again. Why not? I was not satisfied with the lack of harmony between two ways of looking at electricity and magnetism. Michael Faraday had discovered that moving magnets produced electricity in coils of wire. It was the basis for the principle of the generator or dynamo; today falling water moves magnets through coils of wire from which the generated electricity is carried afar. Hydroelectric dams. The theory was based on the realization that the motion of a magnet produced electricity, as discovered by Faraday. If, therefore, a magnet were at rest, then, in principle, no electricity could be generated. But this was patently false, for experientially it was possible to create electricity by moving electric coils over fixed magnets. The phenomenon, as I called it, was only dependent on the **relative** motions of the magnets and the coils. Electricity was generated if either one or both were moving. This was a source of my idea of what became relativity, since it started in that paper of 1905 that began with what I saw as an asymmetry between a theory and an experiment. This aesthetic problem was resolved by eschewing the concepts of absolute motion and absolute rest, and replacing them with the relativity of **all** motion. The next thing to go was absolute time, then absolute space, and, well that's the whole history of my theory of relativity, up to today with the last asymmetry still not resolved between electricity and gravity.*

Oh, Michele, you were there almost at the start: my sounding board who, as I recall, helped me with that initial realization that time itself is relative – a crucial breakthrough in that first relativity paper. Then, at the very end of the paper, I thanked you, and only you, who "steadfastly stood by me in my work," and, therefore, "I am indebted to Besso for many a valuable suggestion." Indebted, indeed. It, in time, changed my life. I keep coming back to this today, don't I? But you minimized your contribution. You used a metaphor: you said you were a sparrow borne aloft on an eagle. Wow, me, an eagle. Better than the donkey, as I often called myself. Strange, how we use animals to symbolize ourselves.

*Am I reading Michele's mind, now? He is looking at my books. He stops at my little book on relativity. I wrote him when I was contemplating that book. I told him that I felt I had to write a popular book because there was already much confusion about what the theory was and what it meant, and I wanted there to be a comprehensible account from my viewpoint, especially because the theory basically is quite simple. Ah, Michele continues wandering around my study. Stops at the record player on the large table, looks the Mozart album cover. The **Requiem**, with a picture from medieval art. Why do they do that? Just because the music is a Catholic mass does not mean the image should come from the Middle Ages. Mozart lived in the 18th century, for goodness sake. Michele then looks toward the window, and then sits himself in my comfy chair. He relaxes with a sigh, and peers out at the scene – gazing around and through the large garden, as I have done for how many years now? Um, about twenty years since Elsa and I moved in. Ah, the pastoral quietness, now kept neat and ordered by Mr. Buchanan. Oh, the gardener: we have not finished our conversation about birdhouse templates. How does he know what size hole to drill? When I get obsessed about something, I have a hard time giving it up. Well, in truth, I never give it up. Ah, Michele's head twitches as he spies a little bird coming and going to and from the blue birdhouse – passing in and out of the perfect-sized hole, intuitively drilled by Mr. Buchanan. Besso sighs to himself (out loud): "Safe, safe from predators." Yes, safe from predators, thanks to the* *instinct of the gardener. But we could make this more precise: mathematical, quantitative, you know, numbers and all. I need to speak with Mr. Buchanan. But would the birds be any safer?*

Michele now turns in my chair, faces my desk, and glances over my clutter. He picks up one of my pipes, used as a paper weight on the notes for the condolence letter, and he puts it back down. He opens the humidor, pulls out some tobacco and sniffs it, making a grimacing face. Looking elsewhere on the desk, ah, he spies my class-picture, picks it up, and closely studies it. He seems to be looking for me. Humm, he is taking the systematic approach – using his finger to scan across each row from left to right and top to bottom. Will he give up before he reaches me at the bottom, right? He is on the last row, scanning across to the end, stops, and backs up to me! He laughs, looks at the ceiling, and laughs some more. So, he sees the lone smiling lad. Now he goes back to the picture, and scans over the entire surface again; he looks at me smirking in the corner, and again laughs a hearty laugh. Working his way back into my comfy chair, continues laughing, until, suddenly, he is fixated at something through the window. Staring out the window, there is, in the garden an apparition of a woman, also in a long, strangely colored robe, coming forward toward the glass. As she moves closer, Michele's white hair begins growing longer and longer, his beard disappears, and at the same time his face and body begin a metamorphosis, as he is transformed into another person with a large halo of white hair, who is clearly becoming ...

*Ah, me, yes me. Now I am gazing at the women behind the glass. It is Anna, Michele's wife, the former Anna Winteler, sister of Marie, my first real girl friend, who I dumped – and Anna never forgot the shoddy way I treated her sister, and never forgave me. Now, I see her as **I** sit in my chair. She gazes at me as she mysteriously comes through the glass, walking up to me, while slowly, ever so slowly, removing her peculiar* *robe. Wait! The woman is not Anna, or is it Anna transforming into? Oh, it is, Marie, yes, Marie. Ah Marie, now standing naked before me! I reach up with my right hand toward her extended left hand, and I rise and met her.*

—Albert, yes, here, stand up, and, ah, let me remove your robe. Here, ah, that's better. Both naked, together, finally, after all these years. Let us caress ... sigh. I've been watching you all day as you struggled to write a condolence letter to your friend, Besso. What have I learned about your famed yet sometimes troubled life? Ah, if only you had married me, not that Serbian girl. I could have made your life more oh, yes, my breasts, aah I could have made you happier than ah, yes, yes, keep doing that, aah, and down there too, aah I would have given you the time and space you required, you demanded; your temperament longed for, and the **sensual** *pleasures too, um, yes, oh yes and I can see that over your life, your struggle with your Jewish identity, your involvement in social causes, your relationships with family, friends, and lovers, and especially your many scientific endeavors, there is oh, ah, ah, and yes there too, a little to the left, oh, I mean* **your** *left, ah, yes, that's it, do that again, umm, there is a thread running through your life that everything, yes everything, took a ah, ah, yes, aaaahh took a backseat to physics, yes physics, your real love, the supreme passion of ah, passion, ahhh, ahhhh yeeesss, ummm passion of physics ah, umm . Oh, oh, Albert, oh, what we lost. Yes, lost. Lost.*

—Uh, Marie, you are right. I have become aware of many things in my life today, through my talks with Besso. Even my goodwill tour of America for the Zionist movement had an ulterior selfish motive – it was a means of publicizing my relativity theory. My science was ever present in almost all that I uh, uh, uh, Marie, oh, you naughty little, yes, that's just perfect, do it again, uh, harder, uh well, science was not **every**thing,

but it took up much, well most, of my life and dedication. You might say that physics was my real passion. But right now, this eroticism is more uh, uhh, uhhh, Marie, oh you little witch so maybe I did make a mistake in dumping you. Our life together may have been uh, uhh, uhhh, uhhhh, uhhhhh....

Oy, pressure on my chest. Shit, that was a very sharp pain, enough to wake me. Uh, am I going to vomit? No, I guess not. Not this time. What was I dreaming? Oh, between my legs – dripping, sticky, ah. Well, no *somnium interruptus* this time, I see, um. It's been a long time, a very long time. Humm, not much semen at this age. Just some drips. Not those whooping squirts of my younger years. Remember that time with Marie, when? – oh, that was not Marie, of course not. But I probably could still sire a child. Oy, what am I thinking? Marie, are you still alive? You are just a few years older than me. Where are you?

What else? Ah, Michele, again. Dreaming a sort of stream of consciousness, as I float above my study. What a day, thinking about thinking, about life, and death. And why a naked Anna and a Marie? Did I have some sexual feeling toward Anna, too? Where, in what unconscious depths, did this dream come from? Women I have hurt – a litany. Yet, I have such compassion for people, collectively – so, why did I behave so poorly, and even sometimes cruelly, to individual women in my life? Too late. Unless Marie is still alive? Humm, my sister Maja's real name was Maria, but we seldom used it. Is that why I dumped Marie? Was the sound of her name too similar to Maria? Some incest thing? Oy, what thoughts I am having today. You would think that I have been reading deeply into Freud lately, rather than mainly manipulating tensor calculus equations.

Ah, Albert. Do you not see that there was an erotic component in your attraction to physics? Let me quote from your Glasgow lecture of 1933 on how you created general relativity. You spoke in carnal semantics about "the years of anxious searching in the dark, with their intense longing, their alternations of confidence and exhaustion and the final mergence into the light." Was this about an equation or a lover. The uninformed listener could not tell the difference, eh? Listen to your language: It could be about sex; even, perhaps, an orgasm? No? Yes? Who knew that physics could be sexy?

Ah Besso, yes, you may be right. Ah, friend, you started all this. Wandering through my study. Perusing my pictures, my books, my desk, my records, the class-picture of the smirking little me with the solitary, impish smile. Fortunately, Michele, you are dead. Released from this vale of tears, free of pain and worry. I'll soon follow you, old friend. Not long. Release me.

Oh, yes? What was it that Spinoza said about death? "A man who lives by the guidance of reason thinks of death least of all things." I surely have been a man of reason. True, I did not think much about death until recently. What was it I said in a letter last month? To one bent on age, death will come as a release. I feel this more so since I have grown old and now regard death like an old debt, at long last to be discharged. At the same time, I instinctively do everything possible to postpone the final settlement. It is part of the game nature plays with us. And so, I am now obsessed with death. Constant thoughts of my demise. Come, come on, death-thoughts, mortality, come, put me back to sleep – yes, eternal sleep. Take me to the place I was before I was born. Remember that? Of course not; what is there to remember? Yet, in a sense we can conceive of it, can't we? Eighty years ago, where was the *I*? The ego. The self. The me. Ah, in a place with no pain, no trouble, no strife, no anything. Just pure unadulterated nothing. Nothing, yes, nothing not empty space – I should know about this, for God's sake. Ah, back to the real nothing. *Real* nothing? – a contradiction? Well, maybe not.

Michele, best friend, could we have that hearty laugh together? Could we laugh and chitchat again? Ah, an afterlife, but I don't believe in such a state of being – it does not fit with Spinoza's God. Oh, well. Then again, I was often surprised in life. Maybe I could be surprised in death. After all, I was frequently wrong about a lot of things. Um, Elsa was glad to remind me of that now and then. So, perhaps, perchance, uh, eh Michele?

Ah, I forgot to show Miss Dukas my class-picture. Should I awake her? No, not necessary. Wait 'till morning. Will she find me in the picture? Of course – me, the solitary lad with an impish smile. I like the sound of that, um. That's why I keep repeating it. We should have a good laugh together. I always liked Dukas's distinct laugh. Yesterday, she and Margot were giggling together. They would not tell me what about, but they kept saying the phrase, "playing Canasta at Hadassah," over again, and then gigging. What does it mean? If I knew, maybe I could write a poem about it; one of my doggerel verses.

Ah, yes, me, here in my hen house. Um, and that pressure cooker episode this morning. I don't think I ever heard Dukas laugh so hard. Maybe that's what woke me up, not the stew shooting to the ceiling. Looking forward to tomorrow, we'll have a good laugh. Humm, did I have the last laugh? Oh, I forgot to look for the birthday package from Otto on the piano bench. Tomorrow. So forgetful. Time seems to be running out on me. Did I truly say that? I who changed the meaning of time itself, am now being beset by the very thing creeping up on me – as I foresee, and very much look forward to, my final end. Time? Illusion? Yes. So *there* Besso! *So there*!

What is in that package from Nathan? I, who need nothing more, except time, huh? Humm, what could it be? I need to get to sleep. What else shall I contemplate to lull me back to sleep? Physics problems? No, they usually keep me awake. My provocative ideas about society and politics? No, too emotionally charged. My struggle with my Jewish identity? That's been settled, I am content in my ethnic identity. Ah, all the women I have known. Yes? Well, no. They may arouse me in ways that will keep me from falling asleep, all night. And, anyway, I already have the sticky stuff between my legs. Oh, well. Ah, let me get up again, and go back to my study.

Sigh.

Ah, my cluttered desk. Oh, yes, the draft notes for the letter to Besso's son and sister. Why not finish it now? Ah, take my notes and write out the final copy of the condolence letter. One sheet of stationery will suffice. Humm, that rain does not want to stop. Coming down strong. What a wet day it has been. And tomorrow? Dukas will probably get soaked walking this letter to the mailbox. Ugh, a sharp pain in the abdomen. Oh, aneurysm, give me time – ah, yes, time – to finish this letter. At last, now? Yes. Ah, okay, here goes…

Princeton 21 III 55

Dear Viro and Dear Bice!

It was so nice of you to remember me, …

" 'Is this supposed to be an obituary?,' the astonished reader will likely ask. I would like to reply: essentially, yes. For the essential in the being of a man of my type lies precisely in *what* he thinks and *how* he thinks, not in what he does or suffers."

A. Einstein.

—An aside from Einstein's autobiographical essay, drafted in 1946.

Afterword

Albert Einstein died in Princeton Hospital on April 18, 1955 at 1:14 a.m. of a ruptured aortic aneurysm.

Otto Nathan was the sole executor of his will. In his will, Einstein left $20,000 to Helen Dukas and $20,000 to Margot Einstein; Margot also got the house on Mercer Street. Hans Albert got $10,000 and Eduard $15,000.

In the will, Einstein also directed all his papers, correspondence, and material related to his life and work ultimately to be given to the Hebrew University of Jerusalem.

Dukas and Nathan were co-trustees of his estate, and as such they had total control over the literary estate in the short term. After Einstein's death, Dukas and Nathan together worked diligently to prevent documents from being released to the public that were deemed by them as revealing what they considered to be the less-than-noble side of Einstein's character (such as the existence of Lieserl).

Then, on a dark night in December, 1981, shortly before Dukas's death, Israeli soldiers arrived in a large truck at the Institute in Princeton, and all of Einstein's estate was moved out in crates. The next day the estate found its new home at the Hebrew University of Jerusalem, where it remains today.

Nathan died in January of 1987. Later that year the first volume of *The Collected Papers of Albert Einstein* was published, containing extensive documentation of the early years (1879-1902), such as the relationship between Albert and Mileva, and all we know about Lieserl.

David R. Topper

The dedication reads:

To the memory of
Helen Dukas
and
Otto Nathan

Ah Besso, do you see the irony? Or is it a double meaning? Some memorials are masquerades for "Oy, good riddance." What do you think, old friend? What? How do I know about this dedication? Where am I? Humm, good question. Where am I? Yes, indeed, where?

* * *

I could have begun this novel, like many a movie I have seen, with this notice:

This is based on a true story.

Some scenes are based on real events, but with imaginary dialogue. Yet, many passages *are* from documented sources. All the people who appeared in this novel were real – except for Mr. Buchannan, who materialized in my imagination, along with Mr. Hans, who supposedly worked in Einstein's father's business. Oh, yes, and the possible names of the lads in Albert's class-picture. It is, in short, a work of historical fiction.

Einstein's dream of the HUAC hearing is loosely based on excerpts from the transcript of the hearing of Bertolt Brecht on October 30, 1947. https://en.wikisource.org/wiki/Brecht_HUAC_hearing_(1947-10-30)_transcript

FYI: Here are dates for the major persona
(asterisks mean they are on the book's cover):

Anna Winteler Besso (1872-1944)
Michele Angelo Besso (1873-1955)
Helen Dukas (1896-1982) *
Albert Einstein (1879-1955) *
Eduard (Tete) Einstein (1910-1965) *
Elsa Löwenthal Einstein (1876-1936) *
Hans Albert Einstein (1904-1973) *
Hermann Einstein (1847-1902)
Ilse Einstein (1897-1934)
Maria (Maja) Einstein (later Winteler) (1881-1951)
Margot Einstein (1899-1986) *
Mileva Marić Einstein (1875-1948) *
Pauline Einstein (1858-1920)
Otto Nathan (1893-1987)
J. Robert Oppenheimer (1904-1967)
Jost Winteler (1846-1929)
Marie Winteler (later Müller) (1877-1957)
Pauline Winteler (1845-1906)

***

David R. Topper

Further Readings?

Much of what is true about Einstein's life can be found in my other books:

Quirky Sides of Scientists: True Tales of Ingenuity and Error from Physics and Astronomy (Springer, 2007); *How Einstein Created Relativity out of Physics and Astronomy* (Springer, 2013); and *Einstein for Anyone: A Quick Read* (Vernon Press, 2015; revised second edition, 2016). If you want to know more about Cantor and transfinite numbers, there is a chapter on this in my book *Idolatry and Infinity: Of Art, Math, & God* (2014). Okay, I know: three books on Einstein are enough of self-promotion. But I have a soft spot for my little book on *Idolatry and Infinity*, which has been widely ignored because it is on the borderline between the humanities and the worlds of science and math. As noted in the novel: a book containing real math scares off the humanists and a book with … well, if you've just read this novel, you know the rest. Hence, every chance I get, I put in a plug for my lonely little book. So there!

Ah, what? More dry, academic books? Who needs them, eh? As I was saying...

Hey, who *are* you? Where did you come from? Scat!

Acknowledgments

I owe a bouquet of gratitude to Sheilla Jones, author of *The Quantum Ten: A Story of Passion, Tragedy, Ambition and Science* (Thomas Allen, 2008). A former student of mine, with a Master's degree in physics, Sheilla is a journalist, historian, and author of murder mysteries. She was the first person to read completely an early draft of this book, and she generously made truly valuable suggestions that helped me mold it into the work it is now.

The second reader was my son, Romi, who helped me find my many typos and such in the penultimate draft.

Special thanks also to Barbara Wolff, now retired from the Einstein Archives in Jerusalem, for her prompt, informative, and warm responses to my many queries over the years. But she may not approve of this book, since she has an aversion to historical fiction.

And, quite possibly, deep in my sub-conscience, I was influenced by the marvelous book about the fictional character Victor Jacob, but based on footnoted historical facts: Russell McCormmach's, *Night Thoughts of a Classical Physicist* (Harvard, 1982). Russ is a friend and was a fellow graduate student in the history of science at Case Institute of Technology (as it was then named; it is now Case Western Reserve University).

Finally, speaking of Case, if I had not taken Martin J. Klein's captivating graduate course, "Some Conceptual Developments of Modern Physics" in the fall of 1965 term, this book surely would never have existed – nor would my life have gone the way it did. Hence the dedication, in the front of this book, to him.

Nonetheless – and, of course – all critical slings and arrows found herein must be aimed squarely at Yours Truly.

On Sale Now!

A DANGEROUS LAND TRILOGY
BOOK 1

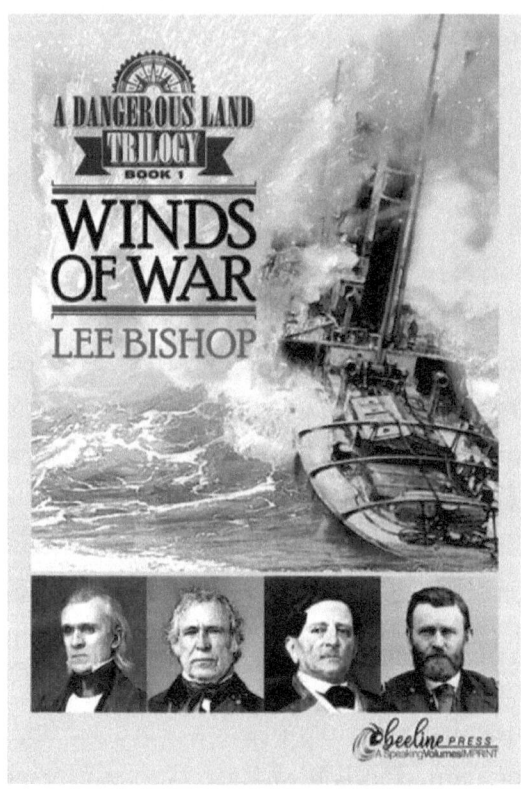

For more information
visit: www.SpeakingVolumes.us